ME AND MY
SO-CALLED FRIENDS

SHARON NEISS ARBESS

ISBN 978-1-77210-042-6

Printed in the U.S.A
Ahava Chai Publishing, October 2015
Cover Design: Josh Arbess

For Carrie

Chapter 1

My body slammed into the window as the camp bus turned a sharp corner into the parking lot of the Cavendish Mall, the neighbourhood shopping centre in Montreal, Quebec where I spent most of my Saturdays. I smiled as I returned to my familiar place.

I rubbed my eyes and thought about the last three hours. I was seat hopping, exchanging bus letters, and even manicuring—which masked the smell of a combination of sweaty gym socks and the stuff they spray in bowling shoes. And of course, how could I forget the first ten minutes of the bus ride—when I was drying my eyes and honking my nose in camp toilet paper after saying goodbye to my friends who lived in different cities.

As soon as the bus came to a stop and the doors opened, a herd of eager parents came running. Then came the shrieks of the younger kids seeing their parents for the first time since Visitors' Day. I winced from the high-pitched sounds as I collected all of my gear and waited in line to get off the bus.

As I headed toward the front doors, in one hand I held my tear-soaked bunk notes and a plastic bag filled to the brim with arts and crafts projects. In the other hand I held my stuffed-to-the-brim knapsack—which should have been on my back — while my now numbing fingers were intertwined with my tennis racquet strings.

Once I hit the platform, I searched through the hundreds of anxious parents and spotted my mom.

"Hi!" I shrieked as I waved my left hand, which was much lighter due to the arts and crafts paraphernalia.

"Hey Lizzie!" my mom exclaimed as she opened her arms to hug me. "I missed yoooouuuuu!!!" And on that last "you," she gave me a tighter squeeze.

My real name was Elizabeth, but everyone called me Lizzie. I decided that when I got older, like 18 or something, I was going to become Liz. Ms. Liz Stein. But for that present time, I just wanted to be Lizzie.

"I missed you too! Where's Dad?" I asked as I squeezed back.

"Looking for your bags, of course!" my mom said, with her hands waving up in the air. She always did that when she spoke, which was kind of annoying but forgivable because she was my mom.

"Okay," I said. "I'll go find him."

My mom took most of the things that were draped on my body, and I ran to where the duffle bags were piled. There I saw my dad searching for my two needles in the haystack.

"Hey kiddo, you look great!" We hugged. "Where are your bags?" he asked in frustration.

I shrugged my shoulders.

After a whole half hour, we finally found my bags.

I climbed into my parents' car and ran my hands over the leather upholstery and inhaled the Stein aroma—a combination of men's cologne, ladies perfume, and fluoride treatments since my parents were both dentists.

"How was colour war?" my dad asked.

"How is Emily doing?" my mom asked.

"Would you like to visit any of your camp friends this year?" my mom asked, even though I hadn't answered her previous questions or my dad's either.

How could I? I was far more interested in looking outside my window because it had been two whole months since I saw Fleet Road and the super-clean streets of Hampstead. I admired the maticulously planted flowers and manicured yet lush lawns. I just wanted to climb out of the car and run through the grass with my bare feet.

Hampstead: A suburban town in Montreal where there are parks, arenas, and houses that range from very small to obnoxiously huge — just like the people who live there.

As we drove up to our house, which is somewhere in the middle between very small and obnoxiously huge, I jumped out of the car before my dad came to a full stop. "Lizzie!" my dad yelled. "Would you at least wait until I stop the car?"

I didn't listen. I got out of the car and dashed to my room, threw off my shoes, and let my toes sink into my beautiful, plush, pink carpet. I walked around my room and gazed at the photographs I hadn't seen in two months, gave my stuffed animals a hug, then said my famous "3-2-1 ooiyyee!" I then hoisted my body onto my bed while bouncing up and down on the bed springs. I maneuvered myself into my favourite "chilling out" position—on my stomach, propped up on my elbows,

3

and swinging my bare feet in mid-air.

After being away at camp, I couldn't believe how much I missed the feeling of being alone in my room. Here, I did what I wanted. Texted friends, read magazines, talked on the phone, or just hung out, without a care in the world. No one bugged me. "Ahhhhh …" I sighed. My mind began to wander.

I thought about my birthday, July 16, which I'd celebrated at camp, and was the best day ever! The camp chef made a cake, threw it in my face, and my counsellors threw a bunk party in the dining hall. I even got to do anything I wanted that day, with whoever I wanted. Of course, I chose Emily, and we had a blast together. We played tennis in the morning, went sailing, and then loafed on the beach all afternoon. "I wish we could do this every day, Lizzie," Emily said to me while we were sunbathing, before I burned my lip to a crisp.

I really hated the fact that Emily lived in New York. We were best friends at camp since we started as Juniors, four years prior. We just sort of clicked the moment I sat on her bed and started to cry because I was homesick. She helped me through it while my counsellor was too busy getting some guy to like her.

While still lying on my bed, I reached into my backpack and searched for the three bracelets I had made for my three best friends from home—Lisa, Amanda, and Gail. They were all in a fishtail design with pink and white gimp. I knew they would love them, because pink and white were our favourite colours.

My back started to itch because of my sunburn, and when I reached around to scratch it, I accidentally unsnapped my bra—which made me think of Lisa. That is how we became friends, because of her breasts.

Back in grade seven, during the first week of high school, we were in gym class and the teacher was having us jump rope. I, of course, never jumped. Fumbling and tripping was a better way to describe my experience that day. Anyhow, I suddenly heard roars of laughter that echoed throughout the gymnasium like the sound of an avalanche. I looked up and saw everyone laughing and pointing their fingers at this blonde girl who was sitting on the floor beside her jump rope, crying. *Ah! The perfect excuse to rid myself of the stupid gym exercise*, I thought. I threw the rope to the side of the gym and ran over to her. She needed my help, and I needed to stop tripping.

"You okay?" I asked.

"No. Get me out of here."

We ran to the bathroom and I barged into an empty stall to snag some toilet paper to wipe her eyes with.

"What happened?" I asked.

"I hate jumping rope," she said.

"Yeah, me too. I can't do it. Keep falling on my face," I said, smiling.

"Oh, I love it," she said. "I jump rope all the time; it's just that today I'm not prepared."

I furrowed my eyebrows out of confusion.

Lisa pointed to her chest, which was way too large for her small frame.

"Oh," I said.

"Normally I put on two sports bras, but I didn't know what we were doing in gym class today."

"I don't think there was a memo," I said.

"You know, when my mom goes spinning, she puts on her biking shorts. I should know what to wear for gym class. They should give us a schedule or something! You know, 'Tuesdays: Jump rope.'" she said between sobs.

"You're right," I said. Let's go and tell the gym teacher."

After drying her eyes and splashing some cold water on her face, we walked back to the gym and told the teacher what happened, and then Lisa was excused for the rest of the period. And so was I! Score! After that day, Lisa and I bonded and became fast friends.

And then there was Gail. Good ol' Gail. We had been friends since we were in elementary school. Always there to talk to. Always there to catch you when you fell. Literally.

For instance, on the first day of high school, there I was, on the bus with Gail, and as usual I was wearing a backpack that was bigger than I was. As I gazed around the crowded bus, I became fixated on a couple who seemed so old—they may have been in grade ten or something. I couldn't stop staring at them because I couldn't believe that they were going to the same school as me. I guess I was staring too long, because the girl got annoyed and barked out:

"Ey!"

"_____."

"Yeah, you!"

My eyes widened.

"Watcha starin' at?"

"Um ..."

The grade ten girl got up and looked me right in the eye. My mouth became dry as sand as I waited for her next move. She pushed me to the floor of the bus. I landed flat on my back and breathed a sigh of relief that my humungous backpack broke my fall. I stared at the ceiling of the bus, smiling because I wasn't hurt but shaking because I was still scared. Everyone on the bus crowded around me to see if I was okay.

"You okay?" Gail asked softly, not to draw attention.

I nodded my head. She helped me up.

"Lizzie, thank G-d you have that backpack of yours!"

"Yeah, totally saved me."

"Wow," a voice said from behind my back. "That was quite a scene."

I turned around and saw a short, feisty-looking, brown-haired girl wearing a very bright, pink shirt with the kind of shorts that I saw on a TV show that I wasn't allowed to watch but did anyways.

I nodded with a smile.

"Amanda," she said as she nodded back to me.

That's when Gail and I first met Amanda.

Amanda always pushed everything to its limit, from her clothes to the way she exercised her mouth. She had guts: she was never afraid of what people thought of her. I totally envied her for that. But I didn't envy her wardrobe because what she wore to school sometimes made me wince uncontrollably. I'd decided that one day I was going to help her with her wardrobe selection, just as soon as I got the nerve to do so.

I'll never forget the time when we all went mini-golfing, but we didn't end up golfing at all. We spent all of our time at the registration desk because the guy who worked there was, in Amanda's eyes, "freakin' hot." I agreed, especially when he tried to speak English with his strong Quebec accent. After breaking the record for lingering,

Amanda let the French-speaking attendant know exactly how she felt, by slipping him her email address.

The four of us were inseparable. We all looked out for each other, especially when we got hurt. Back in grade eight, when Gail had been going out with a guy named Steven Weil for almost six whole weeks, he had the nerve to cheat on her on the eve of their anniversary! Amanda decided to spray-paint "cheater Weil" on his locker. Scared that she might get suspended for damaging school property, Lisa and I went to school an extra hour early the next morning and washed it off. Then, when we got home, we took a picture of Steven, added the caption F%&@-ING cheater, and sent it out to every human being that we knew. See? We looked out for each other.

Amanda only went to camp for one month and then went to Nova Scotia to visit her cousins, so she wasn't due to come back to Montreal until after Labour Day.

I texted Lisa.

"You home yet?"

No answer.

I tried Gail.

"I'm home! You?"

Nada.

I made a frown.

Although I wanted to see my friends, spending the last week of summer and Labour Day weekend up in the Laurentians was something of a tradition in my family, and I couldn't wait to head up there. We could have driven straight up from camp—it was just that my parents had booked two oral surgeries that couldn't wait. If it hadn't been for those patients' laziness at flossing, I could have been reading in our hammock by the lake.

Then again, I did have loads of laundry to do. So I hauled my duffle bags to the laundry room to get started. Just as the washer finished one load and I had started to load the dryer, in walked my brother, Lee.

"I'm back," he said as he opened up his arms to hug me.

"Hellooooo!" I said, looking up at him. "Did you get taller, again?"

"Nope. Still six-two."

Lee was twenty, in his third year of McGill Commerce, and planned to go into accounting. So far, his whole educated life had been annoyingly perfect. Lee had graduated from a fancy a private school for boys that was recommended by his preschool teacher because she felt that he had a gift for numbers at the age of three—a story that my parents LOVE to tell.

In my world, the math thing was most annoying. Why? For as long as I could remember, whenever I had to solve a problem in every math class that I ever took, my shoulders got all tight, my breathing became heavy, and I got a headache. Sometimes my stomach would grumble, but that would only be right before lunch—probably because I was hungry. As I walked ever so slowly (I was in no rush to go) towards my math class, year after year I would whine about about Lee hogging all of the strong math genes in our family. So totally unfair..

Lee had tons of trophies and ribbons for winning every math competition known to man. He also got the Governor General's award for math when he graduated high school. If you ever wanted to know the tip on a restaurant bill in three seconds flat or the circumference of a *McDonald's Big Mac*, Lee was your guy.

Sigh.

Lee was also obsessed with hockey. He played for McGill, and he also played for fun. If he wanted to, he could have probably played in his sleep. Of course, his room was covered in hockey paraphernalia. "Don't touch my walls!" he always said to Mom when she complained that he was wrecking the paint with his posters and hockey shirts. His coach said that he was good enough to go professional, but Lee still chose to go to the accountant route.

Math and hockey superiority aside, I knew that Lee looked out for me. For instance, when I was in grade six, there was a guy in my class named Scott Smith who kept calling me a fat tub of lard. Nice, eh?

Scott yelled fat tub of lard everywhere. In the morning, before I even got a chance to take off my coat, there he was at my locker: "You fat tub of lard!" At lunch, before I took my first bite of my beloved tuna sandwich, there he was right in my face: "You fat tub of lard!" While we played volleyball, as Scott was getting ready to serve: "Heads up, you fat tub of lard!"

Lee had enough of me crying about it at home, so one day after school he took me to Scott's house. I hid in the bushes and watched while Lee marched right into the Smiths' home, pushed Scott's parents aside, grabbed Scott by the shirt, and yelled, "Let's call it quits on annoying Lizzie, okay?" Scott's face turned purple and mine was as bright as the sun. For the rest of the day, along with a case of 'after shock feeling fabulous' shivers, I was so proud that Lee was my brother and that he stood up for me.

The only real annoying thing Lee ever actually did to me was, when I complained that my jeans were getting too tight, he would say:

"Get off your lazy ass and move."

"Move in what way?"

"Run."

"No way."

"Mph."

Was I fat? I wasn't threatened to become a diabetic. Just enough for my family doctor to say, "Can you cut down a little bit on those cookies?"

"It's M&M's," my mother would pipe in.

I shrugged a half smile in my hospital gown.

Or for my friends to say, "Stop stretching out my jeans!"

Or the fact that I couldn't run a mile if you paid me.

I knew that I needed to get out and run and put down the M&M's.

I just wasn't ready. Yet.

Another annoying thing about Lee was that, in my parents' eyes, he was as close to perfection as you could get. "Great idea, Lee," they would say. And: "Never thought about it that way, Lee." And the best: "Lee, watch out for your sister." Could he be any more annoying? Back to the laundry room …

"So ... any hot romance this summer?" he asked, smiling.

"Paul Liss," I shyly said.

"Paul Liss?" he yelled. "Total dork. Total puck hogger when we play his team!"

"Yeah, he also hogged most of the girls in the camp play, after we'd been going out for, like, eighteen and a half whole days!"

"No!" Lee said.

"Yeah!" I yelled. "Stupid Julie Mornstein with her short shorts that showed everything." And then I added shyly, "While my shorts showed

... well ..."

Lee smiled and shook his head.

* * *

The next day, just as I finished packing for the Laurentians and was zipping up my bag, the phone rang.

"Hey ... got your text but I wanted to hear your voice!" Gail said.

"How was your summer?" I asked.

"Amazing!" she giggled. "Get this: We got caught for smoking!"

"You what? Since when do you smoke?" I asked.

"Oh, I just tried it a few times. No biggie. We just had to call home. And I almost got sent home, but luckily my parents just made me do dishes for a week."

"Wow!" I said.

"Yup." she said.

"Okay, so come over now!" I demanded.

"Oh, I have to go shopping with my mother for new running shoes."

"Oh come on!" I cried. "The sneakers can wait!"

"The minute I got home, my mom threw my running shoes into the garbage," she announced.

"So?"

She didn't answer.

"Okay," I said sadly, "so I'm going up north, so I guess I'll see you when I get back."

"Bye... have fun," Gail said and hung up.

I thought about the stupid sneakers. I would have run barefoot to see her. I didn't get it. I sighed and put on my iPod.

Chapter 2

We drove to the Laurentians and arrived just before dinner. We shared our country house with the Goldbergs, who had two kids the same age as Lee and me: Allan and Jennifer. Us four kids slept up on the top floor in bunk beds while the parents each had their own room on the main floor. There was a Ping-Pong table in the basement and an old pool table that smelled of mildew. Even though one of the legs was broken off the pool table, we still managed to play, with the help of an old broomstick. The best part about sharing the house with the Goldbergs was that the parents had this "happy hour" time at about five o'clock when they ate green olives and drank Chardonnay and left us kids alone.

Jenny was in our room unpacking. I reached out my arms.

"Hey ... how was it?" I asked.

"Lizzie, I can't feel my fingers anymore," she said as we hugged.

"Don't your hands get stronger?" I asked.

"I guess. They just hurt now. It was really intense."

"Well, was it at least fun?" I asked.

"Oh yeah, there's nothing like music camp," she proudly said.

I could not relate. Jenny had spent her summer at a music camp, where besides doing the regular camp stuff like swimming and baseball, she also studied music history and played piano for hours a day. During the year she went to an all-girls school that had the best music program in the city. So, Jenny mostly kept to herself and hung out with her music friends. I used to love watching everyone's facial expressions while she played the piano. When Jenny played, the whole room stopped.

Her brother, Allan, was the perfect match for Lee. He was totally into the hockey thing, the McGill thing, the math thing, and, oh yes, the annoying thing—especially his mouth, which sometimes got a little out of control.

"Okay kiddies ... dinner!" Mr. Goldberg yelled. I could smell the barbecue chicken, and my mouth began to water.

I grabbed my seat near the window—my seat for the past ten years.

Allan grabbed an ear of corn.

"Shit!" he yelled.

"Allan!" his dad yelled back.

Allan had a terrible habit of swearing. A lot.

"It's hot," he said.

"Okay, so say, 'Sugar, it's hot,'" his mother corrected.

"I'm not going say, 'Sugar'!" he said. We all couldn't help but laugh.

"Why not?"

"Because I'm not! What's the big deal? Shit is just a word."

"So is sugar." Jenny piped in.

"You just keep your attention to that piano," Allan shot back.

I felt a twinge of sadness for Allan. Must be hard growing up beside Jenny's spotlight. I sighed. I totally related.

"What are you sighing about?" Allan snapped.

I glared at him.

"Leave her alone," Mrs. Goldberg said.

"Just stop it," I said. "Your swearing pisses your parents off."

"Butt out," he said.

"I tried," I said, as I reached out my hand to grab some corn. The eight of us ate in silence for a while, and then my mother decided to tell us a story about how one of her patients improved her receding gums by switching to a softer-bristle toothbrush.

Chapter 3

The next morning, I awoke to:

"Lizzie, get up!"

"Why?" I asked. I rubbed my eyes to focus on my night table clock. It read 7:56 am. "Okay Jenn, it's waaaaay too early!" I said.

"He's here!" Jenny shrieked.

"No way," I said.

"Yes way, now get up and get your suit on! He's on our front porch!"

I slipped on my suit and an extra-long T-shirt to cover my M&M-nourished body.

It was Sam Green. Yes, my crush for as many years as I could count. His family had a country house on our lake, and he used to go to my school. Just writing his name in my notebooks at school made the little hairs on my arms stand up. SamGreenSamGreenSamGreenSamGreen, I would say over and over again. I used to fantasize about what it would be like to have his strong arms hold my waist while his beautiful lips gently press on mine.

We quickly made a mad dash to the bathroom. Jenny brushed her long, super-straight brown hair, and I tried to tame my monster of frizzy curls by spritzing them with water. After we brushed our teeth, we went downstairs and said good morning to our families, swishing by them while they ate breakfast. "Where's your train?" Mrs. Goldberg asked.

Lee was sitting on the porch with the sports page. And sitting across from him was Sam Green. There he was, sitting on an old yard chair, looking as stunning as stunning could be. Jenny and I just stood there, not saying anything. I finally waved hello.

"Hi," Sam said calmly, ever so cool.

"Sam and I are going water-skiing," Lee announced.

"Oh, okay," I said.

"Wanna come?" Sam asked.

"Uh, sure." I beamed like a light bulb.

Jenny and I grabbed towels and took our seats in the boat while Sam went for a ski. I wrapped myself in a towel to protect against the wind. As Sam swished through the waves and left a beautiful arc of water behind him, I watched in awe as his strong legs took control of his skis. I couldn't tell if he was squinting from the wind or smiling at me, so I decided on the latter and smiled back.

After a while, Sam motioned to Lee that he'd had enough. As the boat slowed down, he lowered himself into the lake and Lee stopped the motor. All became quiet, and the only thing you could hear were waves splashing against the sides of the boat. While still in the water, Sam asked, "Wanna go, Lizzie?"

"Who ... me?" I asked shyly.

"Who else is Lizzie?" Sam joked.

"Uh ... okay. But I want to start from the dock," I announced.

"Picky picky picky," Lee teased.

"Just drive me to the dock," I said.

From the water, Sam hoisted himself into the boat, and Jenny and I sat there with our eyes and mouths wide open. Lee couldn't help but notice our reactions and shook his head in frustration. I quickly composed myself. Jenny did not, so I finally nudged her in her ribs to calm her down. As he stood taking his life jacket off, water trickled down his body like water over rocks in a stream. It was a beautiful sight.

"Can somebody please pass me a towel?" Sam asked.

No answer. Jenny and I were staring straight ahead. Composed, but not coherent.

"Hello? A towel?" Sam asked again.

Jenny and I snapped out of our trance and I handed him his towel. I wished I were that towel.

Lee drove us back to the dock and got out of the boat, and then announced that he wanted to go wake Allan up for a run. Somehow, he had slept through all of the commotion.

"I drive," Sam commanded. "You spot, Jenny."

While standing on the dock, I took off my T-shirt and put on my lifejacket—as fast as I could, once again, trying to avoid having anyone see me in a bathing suit.

"I, uh …" No words could come out of my mouth because I was too busy choking on my saliva. I hated when that happened.

"What's wrong?" Jenny asked.

"I'm fine," I said, after gaining regular saliva consistency. Jenny motioned with her arms for me to relax. I shook my head. Which meant: How could I?

"I'm ready to go," I announced.

As soon as the boat pulled me up, I balanced myself on the water, and I breathed a sigh of relief. After a couple of spins around the lake, I let go of the rope and sank back into the water. Jenny yelled, "When are you going to ski on one ski?" I didn't answer her because I was too busy being relieved that I hadn't fallen on my face.

We collected the rope and put our skis back in the shed.

"See you later," I said to Sam.

"Yeah, I'm here for another few days, so I'll see you around," Sam said.

"When do you leave for school?" I asked, feeling very proud that I was able to carry on this lovely, meaningful conversation without choking.

"Next week."

I smiled, nodded, and walked back to the house while deciding that Sam made Paul Liss look like a wart.

Chapter 4

Jenny and I awoke the next morning to the sounds of birds chirping and the very loud chatter of our parental units. They were having their morning coffee out on the patio. I decided that it was okay to wake up to Sam Green, but nothing else.

"You fell asleep reading again," Jenny said.

"It was that cool breeze from the lake. I can't help it—it's just so soothing." I glanced down at my blanket and saw my book open on my bed.

"What are they talking about anyways?" Jenny asked.

"Ech," I said. "Stupid politics, I guess."

"Who cares," Jenny said, yawning.

"They are soooo loud," I said as I stretched and gave a generous yawn of my own.

"Might as well get up," Jenny announced as she got out of bed, put her feet into her slippers, and walked to the bathroom. I followed her lead, and the two of us marched into the kitchen. The aroma of coffee, bagels, lox, and cream cheese filled the air, which was the country house breakfast, extraordinaire.

As I was eating my last bites of my bagel and was licking the remaining cream cheese off of my fingers, Sam knocked on our kitchen door.

"Hi!" he said as he walked inside.

I smiled through a mouthful of food without exposing anything in my mouth, which, by the way, was extremely hard.

"Good?" he asked.

"Hmm mmm," I said, still chewing.

He sat down next to me. I swallowed hard and finally smiled properly.

"Up to a little skiing again?"

My face lit up like a thirty-year-old's birthday cake.

"Uh, sure!" I said, half in shock, half excited, and half really nervous. (Okay, that did not make sense mathematically, but as I mentioned before, numbers are not my thing.)

Sam smiled and nodded.

"Just give me ten minutes and I will meet you by the dock," I said.

Jenny and I cleared our stuff from the table and ran upstairs.

"Oh my G-d," I shrieked/whispered. "You have to come with me!"

"Nuh-uh. You have to be alone with him," she calmly said.

"Alone? Wha? How?" I panicked.

Jenny put her hands on my shoulders and looked into my eyes.

"You must relax."

I breathed deeply.

"Good. Now, go get dressed. You can do this. He's just a guy," she said giggling.

I put on my bathing suit with my heart pounding and my hands shaking. I gathered my rat's nest, which is what I liked to call my hair, into a ponytail, brushed my teeth, swigged some mouthwash, smeared on some lip gloss, and then grabbed a towel from the linen closet and wrapped it around my body—wishing that I could ski with it.

Jenny gave me the thumbs-up gesture as I walked downstairs. As I passed through the kitchen, I went by Allan and Lee and two sets of parents who thankfully did not say anything—except for my mother, of course.

"Nice lip gloss, Lizzie!" my mom said, smiling while she mimed putting on lip gloss. There they were once again, those circus-like hand gestures while speaking. I didn't care, because I was going to waterski with Sam. I smiled and walked out the door to greet him.

"Nice suit," Sam said.

"Thanks," I replied.

"Did the birds wake you up this morning?" he asked.

"No, just adults chatting way too early while they drank their stupid coffees out on the patio," I said. "Whoever invented coffee was totally stupid!"

Sam laughed and a light went on inside of me. I kept going.

"I mean, everyone always talks about coffee." I raised the tone of my voice to sound more sophisticated. 'Oh ... let's go for coffee and talk. Let's get up early and have our coffee before we go for a walk.' And what about these stupid coffeehouses with cappuccino, mocha chinos, la la chinos that cost a billion dollars per cup. When is it going to end?" I shrieked.

Sam was really laughing now, and I loved every minute of it. I went on.

"If it weren't for stupid coffee, I would still be sleeping now. We'd all be sleeping now. Isn't that what vacations are for?"

"Yeah, here," Sam laughed as he handed me a pair of skis. "I set them up for you. It's your exact size."

I took off my towel, and somehow I didn't care about the state of my body that moment, which was a miracle. I put on my lifejacket, sat on the dock, and wet my feet so I could easily slip them into the shoe part of the ski. Sam stepped into the boat and started to untangle the ski rope.

"Geez, the skis fit perfectly. How did you do that?" I asked.

"I remembered from yesterday," he said. I smiled.

I grabbed the dock with my hands and started to slide my way into the water, like I always did—but somehow, this time, I was stuck in mid-air. Because of what, I had no idea. I started to panic. I kicked my legs, which were heavy from the weight of the water skis. I started to scream.

"Hey, hold on there," Sam said.

"What is going on?!" I screamed.

"Oh geez, hang on," he said, laughing. "I'll be right back."

"What do you mean? Where are you going? Why am I stuck here?"

My arms were burning from holding up my weight. All I wanted to do was die. What seemed like twenty years later, Sam came back down with my mother.

"Oh my!" my mother said, with her arms swinging. Now, I could not see her swinging her arms, because my back was to her, but I would put money on it that she was swinging her arms when she said it.

"What?" I yelled.

My mother bent down and I heard a snip. I fell into the water.

"Whew ... that was weird. What happened?" I asked. Sam pointed to the edge of the dock, where a nail stuck out. On the tip of this nail, a generous piece of my bathing suit was hung, like a flag. I gasped. I reached into the water to feel my behind, which was bare. I screamed.

"Get me my towel now!" I yelled and hoisted myself up unto the dock, grabbed the towel that Sam had for me, wrapped it around my bottom half, and ran to my room. Sam was calling after me, but I didn't care. I just wanted to get out of there.

I sat on my bed and stared straight ahead at the wall. I couldn't do anything else. I was never so humiliated in all of my life.

"What am I going to do?" I whispered to myself over and over again.

Lee came running up the stairs and knocked on the bedroom door.

"Oh come on Lizzie ..." he said through the door.

"Go away!" I yelled.

"It's no big deal." he said. "You wanted to show him your butt sooner or later. I know you have a thing for him."

"Okay, first of all, it is a big deal, and second of all, I would have liked to kiss Sam first before showing him my butt."

"So you started backwards."

"Oh my G-d," I sighed.

The mathematical genius did not understand the equation: Ripped bathing suit = total and complete embarrassing moment.

Nobody else dared to come into my room and bug me, where I stayed all morning.

"You will look back on this years from now and laugh," my dad said from the other side of the door.

"Do you have a fast-forward button?" I sighed.

Jenny knocked on the door, and obviously she was allowed in.

"We could hit him over the head really hard and then he will get amnesia and forget the whole thing ever happened! I will go and get a really huge pot right now from the kitchen!" She announced with a smile. I gave her an annoying look through my tear-filled eyes.

For the rest of the week, I basically played mouse. The only squeaking I did was when I asked my parents if I could transfer to a high school in the Laurentians, so that I could have all the poutine I desired all year long—as everyone knows that the poutine in the Laurentians is the best.

Sam came by a few more times. I avoided him as best as I could.

Chapter 5

On Labour Day it rained. I didn't do much that day except read my Seventeen magazine ten times. While we were packing up, Jenny told me to call her after the first day of school. She always wanted to know the scoop about my high school, just like I had to know about hers.

That was one Labour Day weekend I would never forget. Ever.

When we got home we were starving, so we dropped our bags and headed for the kitchen. It was the famous "every man for himself" type of meal, because Mom refused to cook on Sunday nights. Mom had her cereal and milk, Dad made a mushroom omelette, Lee made a grilled cheese with tomato, and I made myself peanut butter and banana sandwich. After supper, I organized myself for school: I laid my clothes out and got my supplies together.

I thought about starting another year of school. Grade nine: What would the year bring? Would a teacher read one of my passed notes in class again? Would I manage to run an entire lap around the school in gym class? (I was always the last one to finish.) And most importantly and most annoyingly (is that even a word?) how would I get by in math class?

I could have texted, but I wanted to hear my friends' voices. First I called Lisa.

"Hey!" I said.

"Hey."

"Watcha doin'?"

"_____."

"Lisa, are you on the can?"

"_____."

"Okay, that is totally gross!"

"It's so natural."

"It's so private!"

"Private schmivate. You've seen me naked."

"Totally different. We were getting dressed."

"What's the difference?"

"Oh, never mind. Call me when you're done."

As soon as I hung up the phone, Gail called.

"I'm hitting the sheets. See you tomorrow."

"But …"

Click.

Gail always felt she needed twelve hours of sleep before the first day of school.

I called Amanda.

"Did your boobs get bigger this summer?"

"Amanda!" I yelled into the receiver.

"Whaaaat?" Amanda whined.

I checked down my shirt.

"No," I said.

"Me neither. Hey—I'll see you tomorrow."

"Wait—how was the east coast?"

"The three R's: relatives; relaxation; rode my bike a bit."

"Oh, cool."

"Yeah."

"Oh, I saw Sam Green this weekend!" I sang.

"Oh yeah? How did he look?"

"Ummm mmm!"

"Was he tasty?"

I nervously giggled and said good night. There was no way in hell that I was going to tell her about my bathing suit incident. Didn't want to spoon-feed her that one.

I let out a huge yawn and stretch before climbing into bed. I felt half excited, half nervous, and half very tired. Once again, may not add up mathematically, but it did to me.

Chapter 6

Bump-bump-bump went my school bag, bouncing on my back. I had just gotten off my bus when I saw Lisa getting off hers, so I ran to see her.

"Hey!" I yelled.

"Uh, Lizzie, look behind you," Lisa said as she pointed behind my back.

"Aw geez," I said.

"When are you going to learn to use that zipper on the back of your school bag?" she said. "Come on ... it's not rocket science!" I had this terrible habit of stuffing everything under the sun in my school bag and forgetting to zip it up.

"Yeah, I know ..." I said.

"Awww, come here!" She hugged me. "Oh my God, I saw the most gorgeous guy on my bus ...where did he go?" She feverishly looked around.

"No way, who?" I asked.

"Going to find out," she said. "I think he's new."

"Let's first find out if he has a girlfriend," I said as I started to pick up my school bag explosion.

"Who cares?" Lisa laughed as she handed me all of my new notebooks.

We opened the huge wooden doors to our school, and that huge familiar breeze—which smelled of floor wax, paper, and old gym socks—blew onto our faces. School wasn't my favourite place to be, but I didn't mind being back that morning. Lisa didn't seem to be on the same page as me.

"Don't we pay enough taxes for the janitors to clean up this dump? It stinks in here! Ugh ... I can't believe I am here for another whole ten months! I should have switched to private school. I hear they bake fresh blueberry muffins at private schools."

"Lisa, I can bake you muffins and bring them to school for you." As I said this, I put my arm around her and gave her a squeeze.

"Aw, thanks Lizzie."

Lisa rested her head on my shoulder and we continued to walk through the hallway to our old homeroom from last year to pick up our new schedules.

As we reached the classroom, we greeted Amanda and Gail, who were sitting on the windowsill.

"Girls, please get down from there!" a familiar voice said from behind me. I turned around and it was Mr. Drane, who was head of the math department for the school and head of brain torture for me.

Amanda and Gail got down, which gave the four of us a chance to hug and chat before the bell rang.

"How was Nova Scotia?" Gail asked Amanda.

"Oh you know, R & R & W," Amanda said coolly.

"What happened to the three R's? I asked.

"Relatives, relaxation, and whales. I forgot to mention the whales," she said.

"Did you really see a whale?" I asked.

"Yes, two. A real one on a boat cruise, and my aunt Dorothy," she said bluntly.

The four of us laughed while more students started to come into the classroom.

"Oh come on, she's not that fat," Gail said.

"Gail, the last time you saw her was at my bat mitzvah. That was two years ago. Add about fifty pounds to that."

My heart sank to the floor in fear that the girls would comment on my weight, which they hardly ever did. But once in a while, Amanda would tease me—and this was a prime opportunity, so Amanda fired a biggie.

"You know, you should watch it Lizzie. As you get older, the way you are built…"

I frowned. Didn't say anything. Would have liked to. Would have loved to.

Lisa put her arm around me.

"No she won't!" Gail said.

"Well, typically, women who start out well…. It's all a gravity thing. We're all doomed for the Emerald City."

The three of us looked at each other.

"Hello? My aunt Dorothy. *The Wizard of Oz*?"

"Not funny," Gail said.

"You can't predict the future," Mr. Drane interrupted. The four of us looked at him.

"I couldn't help but overhear your conversation. Older does not equal fatter, and people come in all shapes and sizes. Don't get me started on how women today are portrayed in the media. I am a math teacher, not a psychology professor."

"Hmph," I said, nodding my head.

"No one has the right to tell anyone they are overweight except their doctor," he said, which shut Amanda's mouth good and tight. I decided that Mr. Drane didn't seem so bad after all.

Then the bell rang. We all took our seats and Mr. Drane handed out the schedules. As I studied mine, I saw that my teachers weren't too shabby. I knew that Lee'd had some of them, and I had a few of them the year before. But, of course, I had the math teacher and deep philosopher Mr. Drane for math. I sighed heavily.

Mr. Drane was so thoughtful that he gave us homework on the first day of school. I got home that night, opened my math book, and stared at the number casserole. I felt the panic start to rise in my chest. I just didn't get it.

The next day during math class, I watched Gail look at the blackboard and absorb all of the mumbo-jumbo. Then she got the next week's assignment and started to work at it right away.

"Why? Why me?" My inner voice yelled inside my head in class that afternoon. I could feel my face scrunching up like a raisin.

"Lizzie, are you alright?" Mr. Drane asked.

I looked up, took a deep breath and nodded.

In general, my first week back at school went by fairly smoothly.

It was pretty much the same as the previous year, except that I had different classes and a new locker decorated with way too much graffiti.

We heard from Sabrina Banks, the school gossip, that the cute guy Lisa had seen on her bus the first day of school turned out to be in our grade. He was a transfer from another school, and he was single.

"Background info: go." Amanda asked Sabrina while she was putting on her lip gloss in the bathroom during recess. Gail, Lisa, and I were leaning on the sinks, waiting patiently for the reply.

"My older brother's girlfriend dated him in camp. Couldn't keep his hands to himself—and I'm not talking about other girls. Big time klepto!" she announced proudly and puckered her lips.

"Ahhhh," we all said in unison.

We also found out that he had a habit of putting thumbtacks on people's chairs.

"Yeah, he collects thumbtacks in his locker—that loser," Sabrina proudly told us. "I saw the container myself. And he spends his weekend nights at his parents' hardware store. I've seen him there a few times."

"Yeeeeow!" Lisa yelled as she sat on her chair during third period that day. The thumbtack jerk had a smile as bright as a spotlight.

"What's your problem?" I said to him, defending my friend.

"That's enough, Lizzie," my teacher said.

I pursed my lips together.

That day at lunch, I walked over to where Lisa, Amanda, and Gail were sitting. "Dummm-da-dum-dum," I sang ominously as I sat down.

"Let's nix that thumbtack guy," Amanda said.

"Waste of a face," Gail said, which meant that his good looks did not match his personality.

"Yeah, what should we do?" Lisa asked as she opened her Diet Coke.

I took a generous bite of my tuna sandwich and started to think.

"Lizzie, why do you have to be such an animal when it comes to food?" Amanda disapprovingly announced.

I stared at her in shock as I continued to chew. I didn't know what to say, except that I was really hungry, and I didn't want to say that, mainly because I was in the middle of chewing. Instead, I looked down to the floor and Gail put her hand on my leg.

"Let's get down to business," Gail said. "What should we do?"

"Yeah, my ass is still sore," Lisa said.

The janitor walked by.

"Ah-ha!" Amanda yelled.

"We need to get to his locker," she added.

"Let's take a bunch of thumbtacks and tape it to his lock," Lisa said.

"And write a wicked note," Gail said.

"But not too wicked," I said.

The three of them looked confused.

"What I mean is, let's give him a choice," I said, smiling.

That afternoon, when the final bell rang, the thumbtack guy approached his locker and his mouth fell to the floor. Just like we planned, a bunch of tacks were taped to his lock and next to it was a note that read: "Stick this up your _____ . [Place noun here]"

We wanted to give him a choice. Hey, we weren't that mean.

* * *

Rosh Hashanah, the Jewish New Year, was just a few weeks after school started.

Synagogue that year was typical because, like every year, I didn't want to go. We belonged to a pretty religious one and I could never follow along, let alone see the rabbi, because I sat hidden behind a wooden wall, known as the mechitzah, which separates women and men so there are no distractions from prayers. To keep myself entertained, I made goofy eyes at a cute baby that was next to me. The rest of the time, I thought about lunch.

Thankfully, Amanda and her family were also members of the same synagogue, so we typically hung out together during the breaks. She always made any boring situation more interesting.

On the first day, I was all set to tell her how bored I was, but for some strange reason, this year she was all excited about the prayers and the rabbi's sermon, which I totally didn't understand or relate to. And when I asked her what she thought of the mechitzah, she said, "It totally rocks, man! I can concentrate on G-d and my prayer book, and that's it. What a great invention!"

Talk about guilt! I already felt bad about being bored during synagogue, but watching Amanda love it made me feel like I was eating an unkosher meal like a bacon sandwich with a glass of milk right in front of my rabbi. I took a deep breath, nodded, and smiled while my eyes popped out of my head. *Who are you?!* I thought to myself.

After services, we went home and had Mom's famous lasagna. I looked over some biology notes, took a nap, and then we went to my cousin's for dinner. I stole a seat next to my cousin, Richard, physics major at McGill. Wow, was I ever different from my family, I thought as I sat down next to him.

"How's school going for you so far?" he asked while he ate his honey cake.

"Hard to tell. Only been two weeks."

"Taking math?"

"Have to," I said as I sipped my tea. "Can't graduate without grade nine math."

He nodded as he chewed.

"Is this honey cake denser than last year's?" he asked.

"Can't be dense enough for me. I need to build a condominium with mine."

He laughed. "I can always count on you for a giggle, Lizzie."

"But you can't count on me for those numbers,"

He looked confused. "I hate math," I admitted.

"I hate to say this, but once you have all of your math courses, all of your doors are opened to whatever career path you choose."

"I'm totally screwed," I said.

From Richard's reaction, I didn't think he could relate.

That night I had a nightmare that I was walking along a long corridor and everywhere I looked, a door kept slamming in my face. Slam! Slam! Slam!

Chapter 7

That Monday morning, after the holiday food fest was over, I put on my jeans and couldn't fasten the top button. I shook my head in frustration and threw my jeans in the corner of my room. I sighed as I opened my dresser to put on my 'forgiving' sweatpants.

When I finally got to school and picked up my trail of books, pens, pencils, calculator, and feminine products (OMG!) from my unzipped school bag, David Skinder greeted me in front of my locker with a smile across his devilish-looking face. His arms were rested on his hips. He had a plan, and I knew what was coming. "Lizzie!" he yelled.

Da-da-da-duuuum! Welcome to the David Skinder Spinning Hour, I thought to myself.

David was about five feet, seven and had short, dirty-blonde hair and light-blue eyes that were almost white. He was built like a truck. He told me that he spent hours in his home gym pumping iron. I thought that he experimented with steroids, because it didn't make any sense that he could become that big by working out with weights—but I had no solid proof, because I had never raided his medicine cabinets. Steroids or no steroids, he was definitely the fastest runner in our grade. And man, that guy packed it in! For lunch, he always ate two sandwiches with an enormous container of milk and a banana, and then for dessert he gobbled down a huge bag of cookies. During recess, he always ate those ridiculous 'power bars' that they sold on infomercials.

David was a happy guy, but he also had a mean streak. He loved to make prank calls and send really stupid email jokes. He also loved to pull people's pants down. Ever since we'd met, back in grade seven, David liked to spin me around in the hallways. He loved to grab my arm and yank me around like a ragged old doll. At first it was funny, and then it became annoying. I wondered why Lisa, Amanda, Gail, and I didn't teach him a lesson, like we did for that thumbtack guy. Maybe it was because we had known him for years and he hung out with us, and maybe it was because he was really big and we were afraid of what he might do to us.

Anyhow, that day, I was in no mood to get 'the swing' after the problem I'd had with my jeans that morning, but that didn't stop David. He swung me around at full force.

After I'd regained my balance, I went to my locker, and Lisa, Amanda, and Gail were waiting for me.

"Lizzie, what size are your sweatpants?" Amanda asked.

"Large," I said.

"No, size cow," she said.

Lisa, Amanda, and Gail burst out laughing. I was stunned because I didn't see that one coming. I just stood there and nervously laughed with them and wondered why Gail and Lisa didn't stand up for me like they always did. I collected my books out of my locker and went to my first class. I should have said something smart, but I couldn't think of anything. Instead, I reached into my pencil case and pulled out a bag of M&M's and gobbled them down. Gail and Lisa followed me up the stairs and into the classroom. Amanda went to Phys Ed.

"Sorry, Lizzie," Gail said. "The opportunity for that funny comment was just so … there."

"Hmmm," I said.

"No hard feelings?"

I managed to smile and walk away to the back of the classroom to sharpen my pencils. What, was she stupid?

Lisa followed me. Wrrr wrr wrr went the pencil sharpener. She looked really pretty that day. Her blonde hair was swooped into a ponytail, and I noticed that she was wearing eyeliner that made her blue eyes look like clusters of blue sky.

"Hey," Lisa said.

"Hi," I said.

"Going to Gail's party on Saturday?"

"Yeah, sounds like fun," I said.

"Oh great," she said. "Want to go together?"

"Okay," I said.

"Okay, come over at six. I'll straighten your hair and…"

"Lisa," Gail interrupted, "what time are you planning on coming over on Saturday to help organize the music?"

"Oh geez," Lisa said. "I totally forgot that I told Gail I would come over to her house early to help set up."

"Why don't you both come over," Gail suggested. "It will be fun.

And you guys can spend the night, too."

I made a worried face as I held up one of my curls to play with nervously.

"I will straighten your hair before I organize the music! Get that worried look off your face!" Lisa laughed. I let out a happy sigh of relief.

"Should we invite Amanda?" I asked.

"I think she's going to the hairdresser. She told me that she wants to go curly and I don't own hair appliances for the look she told me about," Lisa said.

Later that day, recess was, uh … educational. I walked over to Lisa's locker, where Amanda and Gail were standing.

"I need to go outside," Lisa said coolly.

"Yeah," Gail agreed, smiling.

My eyebrows lifted up from confusion as I followed them, but then I knew what was coming, because we were heading to the smoking door of the school.

"Okay, I did not do this the first week and that was good, but I can't hold it in anymore," Amanda said as she lit up her cigarette.

"Totally," Gail said, exhaling smoke.

"We were good girls for the first week and now we're baaaaad," Lisa giggled.

The three of them burst into hysterics and Lisa put her arm around me and offered me a puff, but I refused.

"Our Lizzie, she's still a good girl," Amanda laughed as smoke came out of her mouth.

This was the thing: I had tried smoking before and, when I inhaled the smoke, I felt like someone had lit a match in my throat. If I just took a puff and blew the smoke out, I got teased because I "wasn't doing it right."

So I just stood there, like an idiot, with my arms crossed while the girls puffed and puffed and puffed for the whole damn fifteen minutes. I think they had three whole cigarettes in total. When the bell rang, it was music to my ears.

The day got even more annoying. During math class we got our quizzes back, and my score was status quo: Failure! I just couldn't get it. I held my tears back for the rest of the class like I was carrying fifty bricks that I desperately wanted to dump on the floor. As soon as the bell rang, I ran to my locker, where I grabbed my ever-present Kleenex box, especially reserved for math quizzes. Mr. Drane followed me outside after he saw a big tear roll down my face in class. He stood there, watching me. I quickly blew my nose and went back into the classroom.

After dinner, my mom knocked on my bedroom door to see if everything was okay. I told her yes and she smiled. I didn't want her to worry about me. After a while, I barged into Lee's room.

"Don't you knock?" he yelled.

"Oh, sorry," I said with my head down.

"Hey, what's going on?" he asked with concern, but without looking up from his book.

"Bad day," I whispered.

"Go for a run," he said.

"Is that your solution to everything? Going running?"

"Pretty much," he said, his nose still in his book.

"How could running solve my bad day?" I asked.

"You should try it. It always helps me put things into perspective."

"M&M's help me put things into perspective," I giggled.

Lee shook his head in frustration.

Chapter 8

I was starting to feel nervous about the party on Saturday night. I knew that Gail's house was a safe, comfortable place—because I had been going there after school for the past ten years—but something was brewing in my gut.

I thought back to when we were five and I would go over after school. We would watch The Flintstones and eat Oreos and dunk them in milk. Gail's mom would lend me one of Gail's shirts to wear because I would spill my milk and I hated wearing a wet shirt. Then we graduated to Gilligan's Island with crackers and juice when we were eight. When we were twelve, we would rush home and watch our soap opera, and Gail would lend me her shirts again. Not because I spilled my drinks on them, but because I wanted to borrow her cool tops. As we entered our teenage years, I started going over with Lisa and Amanda for sleepovers. And Gail had been to my country house dozens of times. We skied together and watched horror movies at night with hot chocolate and marshmallows. Spending time together at each other's houses was so fun and so familiar, but this time, for some reason, I was nervous.

Maybe I was worried that the party would be like hours of smoke-filled recesses. Then I remembered about Gail's mother, who volunteered for the Canadian Cancer Society. She wouldn't dream of having nicotine in her house. I felt a little relieved, but not completely.

Friday-night supper at the house of my maternal grandmother, Grandma L, was always a warm experience—both physically (she kept the heat in her duplex way too high) and emotionally (she served the best comfort food in the world and was a great listener). I was missing my grandfather, who died two years prior. As usual, we had matzo-ball soup, BBQ chicken, and a blueberry pie for dessert. You wouldn't know that I was nervous about the party the following night, because I devoured all.

After supper, like a bee to a flower, I marched directly to her living room cupboard where she kept her photo albums. I picked out my favourite one, which held letters and mementos of my grandparents' courtship. Looking at this memory keeper was one of my favourite things to do in the world. My grandfather used to write Grandma long, mushy letters while he was doing his residency training at the Jewish General Hospital in Montreal. I would always get so emotional from the whole thing that I would cry, and my tears would splash on the stationery. When that happened, Lee rolled his eyes, my parents yelled, and Grandma's lips got all tight. Her sweet voice turned serious as she yelled, "Get a tissue. Lizzie, a tissue!" Thankfully, she always let me finish reading, but sometimes she insisted on holding the scrapbook herself.

"Oh, I love this one!" I said, pointing to a picture of my grandparents playing tennis.

"Mmm," my grandmother agreed.

"And this letter."

"Mmm," she agreed again.

"Oh," I squealed, "and what about this letter where he writes that he can't stop thinking about you when he tries to catch ten minutes of sleep in a spare bed in the hallway of the hospital! Wow!"

I started to sniffle. My grandmother forcefully grabbed the scrapbook out of my hands. "I ran out of tissues and I'm not taking any chances," she said.

* * *

Party day arrived, with an offer from Lee: "I'll give you a lift to your bash tonight, and I'll even pick you up in the morning."

I furrowed my eyebrows thinking it was too good to be true. Lee gave in with his bribe from mom and dad: "I get the car for the night if I take you." "Ahhh, right," I said.

At six o'clock I marched to the bathroom to take a shower. I put straightening lotion in my hair for Lisa, put on some mascara and blush, and smeared on some lip gloss. Then I put on my jeans—miraculously, they fastened—added my favourite hunter green cotton sweater, and slipped on my sneakers. I looked in the mirror to see my whole getup and thought that I looked pretty good, though I figured I'd look much better if I took a vacuum and sucked out all the fat from my thighs.

"Let's go Lee, before my hair dries!" I commanded.

We zoomed to Gail's house. When I arrived at Gail's eight minutes later (a world record for Lee), Lisa had the hair dryer in her hand, and the straightening iron was all set to go. One hour later, my kinky curls were smooth as the silk on my mom's nightgown.

"Thanks Lisa," I said. "It looks great." I felt my soft straight hair, which hung halfway down my back. Then we went downstairs to help Gail and her mom.

"Nice hair!" Gail and her mom said.

"Wish it was like this all the time," I said as I gave it a stroke.

"We all want what we can't have, dear," Gail's mom said.

"I know," I said as I started to arrange chips and dip in a bowl.

After about twenty minutes, the phone rang and Gail's mom went upstairs.

"Is he coming tonight?" Lisa asked Gail.

"Who?" I asked.

"Jimmy Singer," Gail said.

"Oh, I know that guy ... just can't place his face," I said.

"He was that quiet guy in our English class last year," Gail said. "You know—he was the one who really liked your poem."

"Don't tell her that he liked her poem!" Lisa shrieked.

"Why not?" I asked.

"We think Amanda thinks he's hot," Lisa said.

"Would someone please tell me who he is?" I said. "You know how I hate not matching a face to a name. It drives me bonkers."

"You'll know him when you see him," Lisa said.

"If he shows," Gail said.

At about 7:30 pm, I saw from the bottom of the basement staircase that Gail's parents were putting on their coats. They had dinner reservations at The Szechwan House. My heart dropped to the floor for two reasons. First, because I was really jealous: their ribs were unbelievable. Second, they were leaving. I should have been happy, because I was a free teenager without parental control. Instead, I wanted a mommy and a daddy close by.

As they left, Gail's dad turned to me and said, "Regards to your parents!"

I smiled and nodded, feeling a little worried.

"Oh, don't worry Lizzie—Cecilia, our housekeeper, is here," Gail's mom said. She obviously saw straight through me.

Cecilia always had a habit of falling asleep in her room watching Wheel of Fortune at 7:30 every night.

By 8:00 there were about thirty kids in the basement. Music played in the background, and I stayed in a corner for a while talking to a couple of girls that were in my biology class. They kept looking me up and down, and I could feel their eyes burn right through my clothes. After a while I got annoyed and bored so I walked towards Amanda, who was sitting with David on the couch.

Her hairdresser had done a really nice job with the curling iron, but the rest of Amanda's ensemble was a disaster. She would have been better off wearing a bed sheet. I wondered if she actually owned a mirror. Her jeans were way too tight and her top was way too small.

Amanda's eyes were glazed as she announced, a little too loudly, "I went to synagogue today and it was totally amazing!"

As for David, his mouth was turned up in a half smile. I turned to him and said, "Are you feeling okay?" He raised his hand and nodded his head, staring into space. David usually walked around with a huge smile on his face like he'd just won the lottery. This just seemed too weird.

Then he took a puff from a small cigarette that was obviously marijuana. My eyes widened.

I strolled around the rest of the basement. Lisa and Gail were in a corner, laughing uncontrollably, and didn't even notice me when I stood right in front of them. They too were exchanging puffs from marijuana. *How did this all happen?*

I just wanted to leave, but Lee wasn't coming to get me until the morning. I was stuck, trapped at this drug fest.

Why didn't I want any? After I nearly burned my oesophagus the first time I tried smoking, I vowed to myself that I didn't want to inhale smoke into my lungs, ever again—even if it meant giving up the chance to get high.

I much preferred alcohol, based on a few past experiences with whiskey sours at bar mitzvahs. Unfortunately, there was nothing at this party but cans of Coke and chips. I kept looking through the display of bottles, hoping to find some sort of refreshment, but then Gail walked by and mentioned something about her parents hiding the booze after her brother's last party.

So I sat there, on the couch next to David, joining him in his game of staring. It was super boring, until Amanda started to get up and dance to Pat Benatar by herself. I figured that Gail's mom's music somehow got mixed up with ours. It was quite a show, especially when she started to sing.

I took a deep breath and looked around the room. Someone was walking down the stairs and into the basement. *A-ha!* It was Jimmy Singer. That's who they were talking about. I had finally placed him, and I smiled out of relief. I hated when I couldn't remember people in my grade. I was thinking about the poem I wrote that he supposedly liked, but I couldn't place it.

Jimmy was a quiet boy, one of those smart kids who hung out with all of the, well, smart kids. I wondered why those kids couldn't skip a grade so they could stop showing off and make things easier for the rest of us. Gail and Jimmy went to the same camp, where they were friends—but they weren't friends in school, which was weird. She had invited him to the party because supposedly Amanda liked him, which I thought was also weird. I didn't think Jimmy was Amanda's type, which was usually the kind of guy who had body piercings in interesting places, and/or a tattoo or French accent. I couldn't picture them kissing, and if I couldn't picture two people kissing, I always decided that they shouldn't be together. I thought about it a bit more, and I could picture Jimmy kissing me.

He smiled and walked over toward the couch where I was sitting.

I looked at him.

He looked at me.

I looked at him again.

He smiled.

I smiled back.

"Hi," he said.

I finally spoke. "I know you, but I don't know you."

He looked confused.

"I mean, I know you, but we don't know each other."

He shook his head like he had a bug on it.

I burst out laughing. I couldn't help it. I was nervous, and I was making no sense whatsoever.

"I'm really thirsty!" was all I could manage to say.

"I'll get you a drink," he said, smiling.

After he came back from the bar with two glasses, we sat down and started to talk about the party and laugh at everyone being goofy and stoned.

"You were in my English class last year, right?" I asked.

"Yeah, you wrote an amazing piece of poetry," he said. "I loved it."

"Thanks." I finally remembered the topic of that poem. "You know, I wrote it pretty quickly, right after I had a fight with my brother. I find that when I'm in the moment I can just write and let my pen dance on my paper." I giggled, hoping that I wasn't rambling on too much. I tended to do that when I got excited, and I was very excited.

"You dance on your paper?" he asked, looking confused but very amused.

Amanda came up to us and announced again, in a very loud voice, how much she'd enjoyed synagogue that day. Jimmy looked at her like she was nuts.

And so did I.

Exit Amanda.

"What was that?" Jimmy asked.

"I don't know. She's one of my best friends, but she can get a bit crazy."

"You can say that again."

"So, you go to camp with Gail?"

"Yeah, we've been in the same unit since we were seven."

Eventually we walked over to a pair of barstools, climbed onto them, and sat down. He asked, "Who are your teachers this year?"

"Silverstein for science, Green for English, and Drane for math."

"I had Drane last year. Just make sure you sit towards the back. He tends to get carried away with those chalkboard erasers."

"I hate math."

"Why?"

"It's just so confusing."

"Why? You should look at it like a puzzle."

"A puzzle? What do cardboard pieces with pictures on them have to do with numbers?"

Jimmy laughed, and reached out to put his Coke down on the bar, but he lost his balance and fell off the stool. I sprang off my chair and went to see if he was okay; we both ended up laughing hysterically on the floor.

"That's something that I would do!" I said between giggles.

We both stayed on the basement floor talking and laughing. We continued talking until my mouth felt dry. I asked him if he wanted something to eat, and we got up and walked over to the table where the chips were laid out. While we were munching, our eyes met. I quickly looked away. Then I slowly glanced at my watch.

"Need to go somewhere?" he asked. I shook my head no. A warm rush of heat raced to my head and my heart started to pound. Then I thought about Amanda. She liked Jimmy, and it would be totally unfair of me to hook up with him. But for some reason, my desires overruled my conscience. Gail's mom's voice rang out in my head: "We all want what we can't have, dear."

He walked towards the bathroom; I followed him and he closed the door. We stood across from each other. I suddenly felt embarrassed and shy. Why was I here, in a basement bathroom with a guy I hardly knew? But a very funny, very cute, and kissable guy, I began to think.

I looked around the bathroom and noticed that it was very old, like from the 1970s. The tiles were all moldy, and there was rust near the bathtub faucets. I looked away from the bathtub and met Jimmy's eyes.

He smiled at me.

"What are we doing here?" I asked.

He shrugged his shoulders.

I didn't know the answer either, but I did know that the only place I wanted to be was close to him. Jimmy walked over to me, put his hand on my shoulder, leaned in, and kissed me.

Suddenly, I heard a thump from the door. I pushed Jimmy away and the bathroom door flew open. Five people fell at my feet, one of them being David—and he'd obviously lost his "buzz" from his dope. He held up a condom package and yelled, "Need one of these, Jimmy?"

Roars of laughter came from everyone and everywhere. Jimmy's face fell to the floor, and I felt nauseated. Jimmy then raised his head and glared at David. I looked around for Lisa, Amanda, and Gail, but they were nowhere to be found.

"You're such a shit disturber, David," Jimmy yelled.

"Aw come on, Jimmy, it's just a joke," David laughed.

I couldn't take it anymore. I needed to get out of there. Fast. So, I ran out of the bathroom and up the stairs to Gail's kitchen. I heard Jimmy call after me, but I couldn't bear to deal with him.

I made a beeline for Gail's pantry, where I could hide. I must have been in there for a good twenty minutes, reading cereal and cookie boxes. After I got onto the canned goods, I heard Gail's parents come into the kitchen.

"I wanted Oreos," I said as I shyly came out of the pantry.

"Okaaaaay," Gail's dad said, sounding suspicious.

They looked at me like I was on drugs, which I wasn't—but I thought that they should go downstairs and take a look at their daughter. The three of us just stood there for what seemed like twenty years.

"Can I please use your phone, my cell ran out of juice," I said.

"Why? Is everything okay?" Gail's mom asked.

"Uh, yeah, I just don't feel well," I said.

"Can I get you anything?"

"No, just the phone."

"Too many Oreos, Lizzie?" Gail's dad joked.

I didn't answer, and dialed Linda's number.

"Hello?" Linda answered.

Linda Newfield was Lee's girlfriend for the past two years. I liked her, but she had this whiney nasally voice that could get annoying sometimes. Especially when she asked me too many questions.

"Oh thank God!" I said. And then I whispered, "Linda, it's me. Can I speak to Lee?"

"Yeah, is everything okay?" Linda asked.

"Not really, I need him to pick me up."

Twenty minutes later, I was in the car with Lee. Everything was all blurry due to my mascara running. Lee said, "What doesn't kill a person will only make them stronger."

"Ahhhhhh! It sucks to be me."

When I got back home, I immediately dashed to the bathroom to splash cold water on my face. Then, out of nowhere, I had the urge to run outside, so I quickly dressed into my sweats and running shoes and ran towards the front door. My dad caught me in the entrance hall and said, "You are not going outside at eleven o'clock at night. Besides— since when do you run?"

I shrugged my shoulders, gave a huge sigh, and realized he was right. So, I took off my sweatpants, T-shirt, and running shoes, and I put on my pajamas. I then went into the kitchen and ate the leftover honey cake from the holidays.

I felt like I was deep-sea fishing among the sharks and being eaten alive. On the embarrassment scale of one to ten, this was about a sixty-six.

As I was eating my grandma's honey cake, I felt miserable. Before, it had always made everything okay. But somehow that night, I felt as though nothing was ever going to be really okay again.

Chapter 9

On Monday morning my mother saw me lying in a fetal position on my bed.

"Time of the month?" she asked.

I grunted.

"Take the day off," she said. I took a deep breath of relief.

I just could not face the music that morning. I was dreading running into David and his detective group. Who knew what they were scheming? I could picture it: Instead of thumbtacks on my chair, he would put condoms, and not only would he swing me around the hall, he would also swing me right into Jimmy. I couldn't bear to deal with all of that.

Plus, Amanda! What about her? I basically stole her man. I had not heard from her yesterday, or anyone for that matter. All very weird. Who knew what was in store for me at school that day—so it was quite a relief knowing that I had an entire day to watch game shows and soaps. Monday was my day off from reality.

Then came Tuesday. As I walked from the front doors to my locker,

David, all devilishly looking, was suddenly in my face.

"Lizzie, when are you gonna start zipping up your backpack?"

"Wha?" I said as I whipped around, making all of my books and stuff fly out of my school bag. Then David threw a bunch of condoms to add to my mess on the floor and burst into hysterical laughter.

"Hey, looks like you're on the rag, eh?" he said, pointing to a tampon.

I quickly picked up all of my things and dashed to my first class.

As I was putting my things away in my locker, I saw big-mouthed Sabrina Banks in the corner of my eye approaching me as if I were a huge sale at a department store.

"Eliiizaabeeethhhh!!!" she yelled. I took a deep breath and smiled as best as I could to her, while clenching my teeth.

"You and Jimmy?"

"I really don't know."

"What do you mean you don't know? Oh cut the crap."

"Sorry Sabrina, not dishing."

"Oh come on. I won't tell!"

"Oh yeah," I said sarcastically as I slammed my locker closed and dashed away.

As soon as I turned the corner, there was Amanda, staring straight at me. This day was getting better by the minute. Not.

"Soooo …" she said.

I nodded and smiled.

"Have a good time at the party?" she asked.

"Uh-huh. You?" My heart was going to explode from my chest.

"Yeah, got great weed. Got serious munchies afterwards. I must have put on like three pounds."

"Mmm."

"Ever try it, Lizzie?"

"Nah," I said, in a suspicious way—because she knew that I never did.

"You should. You know, it doesn't burn your throat like cigarettes do."

"Okay."

I started walking to my first class and she followed me.

"You don't have to be scared."

"Uh-huh." I totally was.

She stopped talking, and we walked in silence. When we got to the front of my classroom, I walked inside and Amanda walked off. I took a seat next to Gail, who looked me up and down as I took my seat.

"You kind of freaked my parents out by hiding in our pantry," Gail said.

"Oh, that—well, I had no other choice!" I snapped back.

"You took Amanda's man," Gail said, a little too loud.

"Shhh!" I whispered. "They weren't going out. Besides, where were you when I was being humiliated?"

"Ladies!" my history teacher yelled.

"Sorry," I said.

When the bell rang I tried to look for Lisa, because we had gym class together. I thought maybe she would understand. I finally found her near the entrance way to the gym.

"Like Gail's mom said," Lisa said as she put on her sneakers.

"We all want what we can't have," I finished.

As soon as the lunch bell rang, I grabbed my brown lunch bag from my locker and headed to the cafeteria. I found a table at the very back, where the janitor usually ate. The table was empty, so I sat myself down and ate in silence. I didn't mind it, because I just couldn't deal with anyone. Then, as I was picking up the other half of my sandwich, I suddenly had company. It was the janitor. He sat down to join me, and together we ate our lunch. He had a very thick foreign accent, but I managed to understand that he was from Yugoslavia and that he was eating shepherd's pie. Not a bad lunch hour, actually, after that morning's fiasco.

Just as the bell rang, I ran into Jimmy.

"Hi!" he said.

"Hi" I said. I smiled and walked right pass him to fifth period. I didn't know what else to say.

As I was going home, David grabbed me by my arm and tried to swing me, but I yanked away and he fell to the ground. I reached into my bag looking for money to buy chocolate, but all I found was a loose button.

I thought about the 23 bus—which picked up kids from all the major high schools and dropped off at every major intersection. Every morning and afternoon, the bus was packed with kids, exceeding safety regulations. It was typical to wave to a friend whose face was smooshed against the bus's window. I didn't want to see anyone I knew, so I chose to avoid the camaraderie fiasco that afternoon and walk home alone.

Jenny Goldberg texted me right when I got home and asked: "Did you do it in the bathroom with Jimmy Singer?"

"COME ON, REALLY?!" I texted back.

"Didn't think so. Geez, these rumours are so exaggerated! I'll go and spread the word."

"Thanks Jen," I texted with relief. "So where did you hear this rumour?"

"Gail's sister," Jenny said. Gail's sister went to Jenny's school.

Sometimes I wished that Jenny went to my school or that I could spend more time with her, but there were too many obstacles. First, she lived almost a half hour away by car, and if a car ride wasn't available— due to my parents' work schedule and Lee's generous lift offers (not)— it was two buses and an eight-block walk. Plus, her career as a pianist was really taking off. She was already touring across Canada during most of the summers and playing at dinner parties all the time. Jenny was a busy girl, so a phone call here, email, and texting was basically all I got.

After dinner, the doorbell rang. It was Gail. I was so happy to see her. She told me that she had to talk to me so badly that she'd run the six blocks from her house to mine. Her huge brown eyes looked so sad, like she had been crying. Her straight, brown hair was pulled up in a ponytail, and she was sweating all around her hairline and panting like a dog. We walked to my bedroom, and I flipped on my light, put on my iPod speakers, and sat down on my beanbag chair.

"Are you okay?" I asked.

"I think I was a little harsh in class today," she said. "Jimmy wasn't and isn't going out with Amanda, so ... I don't think it was such a crime to do what you did."

"I guess," I said. I paused, took a deep breath, and asked her the question that was burning in my brain: "But where were you when

David burst in to the bathroom?"

"Too stoned."

I shook my head and frowned.

"Okay, here's the thing. I thought those small cigarettes were homemade ones, not marijuana!"

"Oh come on, Gail!" I yelled.

"Really, my grandpa used to smoke them."

"Are you sure they were cigarettes that he smoked?" I asked.

"No ..." she said softly.

We burst out laughing.

"Look, I would have been there, but I just didn't know where I was, and I couldn't get off the floor."

I took a deep breath, shook my head, and smiled.

"Okay, how was he?" she said, smiling.

"Oh. My. G-d." I giggled. She laughed.

"Okay, what are we going to do about Amanda?" I asked.

"Oh, she'll blow over it," she said, waving her hand in the air.

"You think?" I asked.

"Yeah."

I wanted to ask her about the smoking-at-recess thing, but I decided to let it go. It just didn't seem relevant in comparison to what we were talking about.

"Why did your sister say I had sex with Jimmy?" I flat-out asked her.

"I swear I had nothing to do with that!" she yelled.

I believed her. I had to, because she was my friend.

Chapter 10

"Let's go to the mall," Amanda announced the next day at lunch as the four of us were gathered around Gail's locker.

"Okay," I agreed.

"Was I talking to you?" Amanda barked. Lisa laughed uncontrollably and Gail shook her head.

I stared straight at Amanda and Lisa feeling very confused and very humiliated.

"I think I'll just stay here," I said.

"Yeah, you do that," said Amanda. "Do lunch with the janitor. Again!"

"Ha! Again!" Lisa laughed.

Gail and Lisa followed Amanda to the front doors.

Gail looked back and shrugged her shoulders, and I raised my hands in the air and gave her a look that read: "Why are you following her—especially after our talk last night?"

She read me loud and clear but continued to walk away. After that scenario, I lost my appetite and sat by my locker reading a magazine.

To put a cherry on top of that lovely lunch-time scenario, on my way home from school, I ran into my camp-boyfriend-turned-idiot, Paul Liss. Coincidentally and annoyingly, he lived just a couple of blocks from my house.

"Hey, your brother pulled a fast one on me yesterday on the ice," he said.

"Too bad," I said.

"Yeah, but I heard you made a fast one on Jimmy Singer."

"How do you know him?"

"I have my sources."

"_____."

"Did you teach him everything I taught you?"

"_____."

"Better be careful with your little group of friends," he said, and then walked away.

I stood there at the corner of my street, staring into space, not knowing what to do, feeling very pissed and very confused.

* * *

Later that night I couldn't take it anymore. I didn't want to email or text what I wanted to say. I called Amanda to confront her.

"What?" she yelled. "You're worried that you hurt my feelings because you played kissy face with Jimmy?"

"I feel really bad."

"Naww. I don't care! I'm just screwing with your head. It's fun! You know, you should try screwing with Jimmy. That would be fun!"

"Amanda."

"Ha! Take care, kid. Hey—I'm sorry. Look, I'll stop screwing with you, but you have to promise me that you will start screwing Jimmy."

"Uh, right," I said.

I hung up the phone and realized that I had crazy friends, but at least they forgive easily—or so I thought.

* * *

Unfortunately, it was all going downhill like a black diamond ski hill run. Steep, scary, and tons of moguls. Math was driving me mad. Fear would boil deep in my stomach as I entered the classroom and saw Mr. Drane write down equation after equation and my fellow classmates flipping through their books and punching numbers on their scientific calculators, which by the way had too many buttons for my liking. I would swallow hard and take my seat. My heart would beat fast as I stared straight ahead, trying to figure out what to do with all the problems. The questions never seemed to end.

"Lizzie?" Mr. Drane asked.

No answer.

"Lizzie?" Mr. Drane would ask again.

"Lizzie, can you tell me how to solve this logarithm?" he asked.

"Logarithm. Does it have to do with a tree?" I answered.

Chapter 11

On Friday night, Lisa, Amanda, Gail, and I went downtown to see a movie. As we entered the entrance to the subways, we gave each other our "subway nod." Translation: Each of us rides in a separate car, in search of cute guys. We'd done this ritual ever since the day our parents allowed us the freedom of traveling by subway.

My ride was a quiet one. The only guy I saw was someone who was really old, like thirty or something. As our stop approached, I got off and looked around to find my friends.

"Where's Lisa?" Amanda asked.

Our heads bobbed around, but there was no sign of Lisa. My heart sank to the floor. I grabbed my cell phone. We climbed the stairs to go outside so we could get reception. Lisa beat us to it. My cell phone rang the minute we hit the escalator.

"Where are you guys?" Lisa shrieked on my phone.

"Where are you?" I calmly asked her.

I volunteered to travel back a stop to meet her.

"I am so embarrassed!" Lisa said to me as she opened her arms to hug me.

"Hey, there's nothing to be embarrassed about!" I said. "Who cares? You're safe."

"I know, I guess I just wasn't paying attention to the stops," she said.

"You know to get off at Lionel-Groulx like we always do," I reassured her.

"I guess I got lost in the advertisements."

"Next time, I'm going with you."

"Great. Riding the subway alone sucks."

"Totally."

"And it's more fun to pick up guys when you're with someone."

"Uh-huh." I hung my arm around Lisa and we hopped on the next subway car to meet Amanda and Gail.

"What happened?" Amanda asked.

"Oh, she met a cute guy in her car; got sidetracked," I said.

"Figures!" Gail giggled.

Lisa smiled at me. "Sorry I laughed at you the other day at school," she whispered into my ear.

"Sokay," I whispered back. I couldn't help shrug the incident off.

We entered the theatre and went to the snack bar to get popcorn.

"Watch that butter on your popcorn," Amanda said to me.

"She can have as much butter as she likes," Lisa said.

"I'm just looking out for her," Amanda said.

"She can look after herself," Lisa said as she grabbed her drink and popcorn.

I shrugged and smiled at Amanda.

"Gail, do you want to share a box of Goobers?" I asked.

"I thought you'd never ask," Gail said.

"I'm sure Amanda would like some too, wouldn't you, Amanda?" I asked, sarcastically.

"We can all use some Goobers!" said Amanda, and she took two boxes.

"Atta girl," I said. We all then marched into the theatre to watch our movie.

The next morning, the four of us met for pancakes.

"Lizzie, that's a lot of pancakes," Gail said. "You sure you are going to eat all of that?"

"Okay, what's with you?" I yelled. "Last night you were on my case but then we were all Goobering and everything was cool, and now you're the pancake police?"

"You should start to jog. It does wonders for my thighs," said Gail.

I sat in my chair and my mouth didn't move.

"Yeah," Lisa said.

"I don't believe this," I said in an angry tone.

"We're just looking out for you," Amanda said.

"There you go again," I said. "'Looking out for me.'"

"Oh, poor Lizzie," Amanda said.

"Don't poor Lizzie me. Stop screwing with my head, Amanda!"

People started whispering and pointing.

"Oh, but it's fun!" Amanda said.

"No, it's not." I said, as my blood started to boil.

"Okay guys, calm down," Lisa said.

"You want me to calm down?" I said. "Lisa—think for yourself. Be on my side for once. Reciprocate!"

"Excuse me?" she said, shocked.

"Oh never mind." I said as I got up. I left the restaurant without even paying for my pancakes.

* * *

Just before we were leaving for my grandmother's house for dinner on Friday night, my parents laid a biggie on me—but realistically, I knew it was coming. It was only a matter of time before the rumour spread to the next generation.

"Lizzie, what is this about you having sex at Gail's party?" my dad asked.

"I did not have sex," I said.

"She did not have sex," Lee said.

I breathed a sigh of relief from Lee's comment, but my parents persisted.

"We heard from David Skinder's parents that you had sex in Gail's basement bathroom at that party she had," my mom said.

"Prick," I said under my breath.

Thankfully, my mother did not hear my remark and asked with her eyes glaring and her hands swinging, "Well, did you?"

"No!" I said in an angry tone, looking at both of them.

"Lizzie did not have sex with Jimmy Singer," Lee insisted. "She didn't have sex with anybody. She told me what happened at the party and it was all pretty innocent, if you ask me."

Another breath of relief from me.

"Well, what did happen at the party?" my mother asked.

"Mom, let her be fifteen," Lee said.

"Thank you," I said to Lee.

Lee nodded.

We all composed ourselves and got into the car.

In her soothing "I'm going to freeze your mouth now before I rip out your tooth" voice, my mom said, "You know, we're not going up north this weekend, because of the Smith wedding."

"Oh," I said.

"Maybe we can watch a movie or something."

"Yeah, sure."

"Good," she said. "It's all settled."

I saw my mom smile as if she had pulled out that tooth. She was satisfied.

"You know," I began, "you can all take a huge breath of relief because no one is going to have sex with me once they take a look at my thighs."

Chapter 12

On Saturday, I tried—and I mean tried—to do my math homework, but as usual, I got frustrated.

"Hey, you busy?" Lee asked through my closed door.

"Naw, come in," I said.

"Come on. Get your sneakers. We're going for a run," he said, smiling. I really had no excuse, so I agreed to go.

On top of the regular panting and heaving, I managed to somehow accumulate tons of saliva in my mouth, which I then had to spit out, just like a ball player. I felt like an abused animal. And what did Lee say to my beet-red face after thirty minutes of pure torture?

"It gets better. Trust me."

I raised my eyebrows at him, panting.

After I got out of the shower, I was sitting in my robe in my room when Lee knocked on my door.

"Now what?" I whined.

Lee barged in and said: "Okay, it's time to get serious," Lee said.

"Serious about what?" I asked.

"Running, you varmint."

"Oh," I said softly.

"Really. We need to get you a pair of proper running shoes. The ones you have suck and will screw up your spine and knees. Get dressed and meet me at the front door."

I was stunned. "You're taking me?"

"Yup. Hurry up."

I thought this all was pretty something. Lee taking me shoe shopping. While we sat in the car I couldn't help but bombard him with questions about this running extravaganza I was going to partake in.

"How long have you been running for?"

"Since I was twelve."

"Why?"

"It helps me think."

"Think?"

"Yup."

"Can't you think sitting in a chair?"

"Yeah, but when I run, it relaxes my whole body, all my muscles. All of my tension just melts and my thoughts just appear."

"Oh."

"Don't worry, you'll get it."

"But how do you know that I want this? Maybe I don't want to run and think. Maybe I just want to sit in a chair and..."

"Eat M&M's?" Lee interrupted.

"Maybe."

"Run with me and I will show you a whole world where you won't need M&M's anymore."

I couldn't see how that could be possible, but as we bought a pair of shoes that had really cool-looking aquamarine stripes across the sides—despite Lee's request for bright-orange ones—I became excited to enter into Lee's world of running.

The following Friday at school, something absolutely awesome happened, and it made me forget about everything: from Lisa, Amanda, and Gail making me feel like a fat beached whale to the torturing humiliation at Gail's party. It was this: Sam Green walked into our school. He had come home for Thanksgiving weekend and he decided to stop by for a visit. I nearly fainted when I saw him walk down the hallway. I thought I was hallucinating. But it was he, in the flesh, and he looked even more gorgeous than he had the last time I saw him. When we spotted each other, stupid David got in the way and grabbed my arm to give me a spin. Sam just stood there and watched me go around and around the hallway. I yelled through my torment, "Hold on a sec, this won't take long!"

"And, there you go!" David said as he spun me one last time.

I got up, smoothed my hair, straightened my shirt, and walked over to Sam.

"Hey!" I said, smiling, hoping that my lip gloss was still on.

"How's it goin'?" Sam smiled with his perfect smile.

"Good."

"You look good." He was still smiling.

"Oh, thanks," I said, as I felt my face get very hot. "How's school?"

"Classes way too big, dorm room way too small," he said, laughing. "Girlfriend, just right."

"Oh," I said. Suddenly, I felt six.

We chatted for a little while longer and then the bell rang.

Later, as I entered my classroom still in a daze, Amanda said, "Wouldn't you just love to do it with Sam?'

"Do what?" I asked.

"You know, do it."

"Excuse me?"

"What about Jimmy?"

"What about him?"

"Come on ..."

"For the last time, I did not have sex with him!" I yelled. I wanted to slap her. "What is with you? Why are you doing this?"

Amanda stood there, looking at me.

"You know, he likes girls that go to synagogue."

"I know you liked him, Amanda. He's not my boyfriend. Take him!"

"No thanks," she said smugly, and walked away.

I thought about Jimmy and me kissing in the bathroom. It must have killed Amanda, and now I was being punished. But why were Gail and Lisa acting like idiots, too? One day they were great and the next, horrific. My head started to spin.

David came up from behind me and squeezed my waist and said, "Sure… you didn't do it with Jimmy."

My eyes started to dart around as I tried to process everything. Was David the one spreading the rumor? Was it Lisa, Amanda or Gail? At that point, I wasn't sure what was going on anymore. I just had to run away. I threw my books across the room and ran down the hallway towards the girl's bathroom. I heard footsteps follow me.

"Male teacher entering washroom!" a familiar man's voice said.

I looked up and saw that it was Mr. Drane.

"Mr. Drane, you can't be in here!" I shouted.

"It's okay if I need to be. It's in the school handbook. Page 5," he said, and he grabbed some tissue from a bathroom stall and handed it to me.

"What's going on?" he asked.

"Oh, a stupid rumour." I said.

"About what?"

"Something too embarrassing to tell your math teacher!"

"Oh, that kind of rumour," he said, smiling. "Tell you what. Take a walk to the office, and tell them I sent you."

"Thanks," I said through tears. I walked quietly down the school hallway as more tears ran down my cheeks. I just wanted to crawl into a hole and die.

I opened the huge, heavy glass doors that housed the administration office. Thankfully, there were no students there.

"Yes?" said a lady with a baby-pink angora cardigan. She tilted her head downwards so she could see me through her reading glasses.

I spoke just above a whisper. "Uh, Mr. Drane sent me."

"For what?"

My eyes darted around the office.

"Oh. Please take a seat."

She had obviously seen my wet cheeks; she came over to me with a box of Kleenex and started to ask me stuff, but I couldn't understand her. She then called my parents.

The four of us sat in the principal's office, but I couldn't hear anything. Voices seemed to be in slow motion, and I stayed quiet most of the time.

My parents finally stood up and I followed them outside to our car. We went home and I crawled into bed.

I awoke at dinnertime. My parents were waiting for me in the kitchen.

"Sleep okay?" my dad asked.

"Yeah," I said. My dad motioned me to sit down at the kitchen table, and stood with his hands in his pockets while my mom sat down next to me.

"There seems to be a lot of "stuff" going on with you at school," my mom said.

"You don't seem like yourself," my dad added. "What's going on with Lisa, Amanda, and Gail anyways?"

I swallowed hard.

"Come on Lizzie, you can talk to us," my mom said.

I stared straight at the refrigerator. It was humming pretty loudly. I finally spoke.

"I think I figured out who spread that rumour about Jimmy and me having sex."

"And…?" prompted my dad.

"Yes, it was my so-called friends: Lisa, Amanda, Gail and David."

"How do you know?" my mom asked.

"Just do."

"What are you going to do about it?" my dad asked.

"I don't know."

More silence.

The refrigerator kept humming.

"Can I have a bowl of cereal?" I asked.

"Are you sure that's all you want?" asked my dad.

"Yep." I gave him a half smile.

And that was the end of that.

Lee came into the kitchen. He smiled at my parents and smiled at me.

"Hey, let's go for a run," he suggested.

"No thanks," I said.

"Oh come on. It will be great. It will make you feel better."

"I don't want to," I insisted.

"What happened to those new shoes I got you? You gotta use them."

"I'll use them soon," I said.

"When?"

"Give it a rest!"

"When?"

"Just leave me alone!" I said. I got up and went to my room. Ten minutes later, my mom knocked on my door. She brought me a bowl of Raisin Bran with strawberries.

That night I had a terrible nightmare. I was swimming in the lake at camp, and all of a sudden I heard the theme music from Jaws. My heart started to pound and I started to scream. A shark emerged from the lake and revealed three heads with faces like Lisa's, Amanda's, and Gail's. All three of them opened up their jaws and gave out a roar like a lion.

I woke up, startled and in a sweat.

Chapter 13

Iglanced at the clock. It read 6:30 am, so I got up to take a shower. As I was washing my hair, the herbal scent relaxed me. I took a deep breath and dreaded going to school that morning where I would have to face Lisa, Amanda, and Gail. "Lisa, Amanda, and Gail," I said in my head, over and over, until I created an acronym. LAG. "LAG, LAG, LAG," I whispered to myself.

I towelled off, got dressed, ate breakfast, brushed my teeth, and headed to school, even though I would have preferred to stay home and hide under the covers.

The bus ride to school was peaceful because I had my iPod on and I just tuned out. First and second period were quiet, if mundane. And then, third period: BOOM.

While I was in Home Economics, kneading my dough for chocolate chip cookies, familiar voices echoed from the intercom. At first there were only giggles, but they resolved into the voices of David and LAG.

"What a wonderful piece of poetry!" Gail's voice said.

"So beautiful!" came Amanda's voice.

"So romantic!" Lisa gushed.

We all stopped making cookies to listen.

"'Closer.' By Lizzie Stein," a voice began.

While I stood there, motionless, with my hands in my batter, I felt David and LAG pull out my soul from my body, shove it into a blender, and then hit the "whip" button. My stomach turned a million times and my mouth became dry.

Amanda recited a poem I had written just after Gail's party.

Can I ever be closer?
Can I climb into his soul?
His touch
His warmth
Makes me whole.

My heart sank to the floor.

"And there's more!" Amanda announced but stopped short. "Uh—Mr. Chow!"

"How did you people get in here??!" Principal Chow's voice echoed through the classroom. After the voices disappeared, the whole class was staring at me. My teacher had her hand over her mouth and her eyes were popping out of her head.

With hands full of cookie dough, I ran to the office.

"Who? What? Where are they?" I shrieked. "How did that happen?"

"You are going to have to calm down, Lizzie," said Principal Chow. "Don't worry, we are handling the situation."

"But where did they go?" I said.

"Please, return to your class and we will contact you very soon."

"What do you mean you're going to contact me? Do you expect me to continue the day after that?" I yelled.

"Please, Lizzie, go back to class," said Principal Chow.

Obediently, but very frustrated, I walked back to my class and washed my hands in silence. Everyone was staring at me.

I spent the rest of that agonizing day with my head down, staring at the floor. When the bell rang, Jimmy was at my locker. "Hi," he said.

"Bye," I said. I couldn't deal with him.

When my parents came home from work, they found me lying in a fetal position on my bedroom floor.

"You okay?" my mom asked.

"Not really."

"What's going on?"

The phone rang. It was Jenny. News traveled fast.

"They got detention for three weeks," Jenny reported. And then something happened to me.

My heart started to beat really fast. Mom brought me to the bathroom. I looked in the mirror. I was flushed, and my clothes were soaking.

"What happened at school today, Lizzie?" my mom asked.

"They stole my diary. Read it over the intercom."

"Oh my G-d."

I was breathing hard and I started to cry. I started to wave my hands up and down. Then I stormed out of the bathroom and started pacing in the hallway frantically. My dad ordered me to sit down and take deep breaths, but I couldn't. Lee barged in and asked what all the commotion was about, and my mom told him to get a brown paper bag. Lee came back and handed me a brown lunch bag, but I threw it in his face. I didn't want a paper bag. I started to feel scared. My dad said, "Call 911!"

Five minutes later, three large men came into our house. I didn't even hear the doorbell ring. They had a stretcher, just like on TV, and they asked me to lie down. I couldn't lie down. I just had to keep moving. Two of them grabbed me and forced me onto the stretcher and strapped me in with seatbelts. I tried to kick them off, but they held me down and carried me to the ambulance. I saw out of the corner of my eye that my mother was looking very panicky, like she looks before she has thirty people over for a Passover Seder.

I was carefully carried into the back of the ambulance. I felt my heart beating a thousand beats per minute, and it felt like an elephant was standing on my chest. Could I possible be having a heart attack? At fifteen?

My mind was racing, all the way to my funeral. Would LAG regret all of their obnoxious comments? Would Amanda feel sorry that she spread that ugly rumour? Would David be sorry he constantly abused me? Would they even cry? Suddenly, I decided that the reason I was having this heart attack was because I had huge thighs. Bingo!

As I was thinking about who should get my gold monogrammed necklace, my parents climbed into the ambulance and held my hand. They both looked very worried. I just lay there staring at both of them while we rode with the siren on—wee-ahhh, weee-ahhh—all the way downtown to the Children's Hospital. I prayed that everyone in Hampstead was busy in their homes making dinner and wouldn't look outside to see what the commotion was.

At Emergency I was put into a wheelchair. The last time I was in a wheelchair was when I was eleven years old and I fell off a high bar at camp and landed on my nose. I had gauze dipped in liquid cocaine shoved up my nose, and all I remember is that my counsellor wanted to have gauze dipped in liquid cocaine shoved up HER nose. I thought she was bonkers. I could tell they were wheeling me pretty fast, because I could feel the wind blowing in my hair, and I heard myself going, "Whee!"

I ended up in a bright, huge room with lots of empty beds, and the nurse asked if I needed help to sit on the table. By then I was feeling much better and I told her that I wanted to get up on the table by myself. Nobody was forcing me to do anything, so I started to calm down. I took deep breaths and held my mother's hand while my dad was scurrying about trying to find a doctor.

After about ten minutes, a young male doctor came in and took my blood pressure. He asked me what had happened during the day from the time I woke up. I told him in great detail. My parents kept interrupting, and I finally told them to keep quiet and to let me talk.

Ten minutes later, a woman came in chewing a huge piece of bright-pink bubble gum, which I thought was totally weird. She introduced herself as Dr. Yang, chief psychiatrist, and stated that she would like to do an assessment. She started to ask me basic questions, such as where I lived and how old I was. Then the questions started to get more serious. "Do you have nightmares?" she asked. "How do you handle yourself when you get angry?" I tried my hardest not to laugh, out of pure nervousness, but a couple of giggles sneaked out. She didn't seem to mind. She then told me frankly that I had just had my first panic attack. I took a deep breath and felt the tears roll down my cheeks. I was so scared. She told me that I was going to be fine and that I should follow up with my family doctor as soon as possible. And then she left with my parents to go over some paperwork. She closed the door behind her. I was alone. Lying on the hospital bed, I stared at the mildew-stained ceiling. I stared at the blinking fluorescent lights.

Tears started rolling down my cheeks, but I wasn't sad. I felt somewhat relieved. It seemed that the breakdown that I had cleaned up my soul and took away all of the tension and frustration that I was feeling. I started to breathe deeply and thought about what David and LAG had done to me, how they had been making me feel like crap. I sighed, reflecting on my habit of popping M&M's, my problem with math, and the fact that a very good pair of running shoes was collecting dust in my closet. I began to smile.

Dr. Yang and my parents came into the room. They were all holding coffees. My mom handed me a carton of chocolate milk and kissed me on my head.

* * *

I stayed overnight in the hospital for observation. The next day, on our way home, there was a ton of traffic. Our car stopped in front of an office building, and as I read the advertisements on the window, I squealed with excitement.

"That's it!" I said.

"What's it?" my dad asked.

"Join Frieda's Happy Losers for half price!"

Chapter 14

When we got home, I went to my room and plopped on my bed, which was the only place where I felt truly relaxed. My eyes darted around. I couldn't believe what the past twenty-four hours had brought me. It had been the roller coaster ride of my life. I stared at my phone. Do I call them? Text them? Email? Do I want to shoot them? With what, I thought? The only lethal thing in my house was a garlic crusher. I decided the only thing I could do was let my head fall between my arms and let it all out. Tears came down like rain.

My parents popped their heads in my room when they heard me sobbing.

"I can't go back tomorrow," I said.

"You have to," my mother said.

"Why?"

"It's the law, first of all," said my dad.

"No, seriously. Come on. Just let me have one more day to recuperate," I pleaded.

"If you don't go tomorrow, they will think they've won," my mother said.

* * *

Lee did a good deed and drove me to school the next morning. We didn't talk in the car. I was in no mood for any type of lecture or pep talk. All I wanted was to show them that I was still standing.

As I entered the school and walked to my locker, everyone became quiet around me. You could hear the occasional whisper, but it was as if I was a celebrity or something.

"Boo!" I said and quickly turned around. I startled everyone who was staring, and giggled to myself.

"Hey, where were you yesterday?" Jimmy asked as he appeared behind my back.

My happy face turned flat as a pancake. I wasn't ready to face him yet.

"Uh, sick. Bad headache," I lied and walked away into a corner of the hallway. Of course, Jimmy didn't give up. He followed me.

"Don't walk away from me," he said firmly.

"Why not?"

"Because I want to talk to you."

"About what?"

"That piece you wrote."

I looked away.

"I loved it," he whispered.

"Thank you, but hello? It was private. Not intended for you—or the whole school—to hear."

I started to walk back into the main hallway and ran into Sabrina Banks. My stomach turned.

"Oh, hey. Look at you!" Sabrina began. "My dad saw you being carried into an ambulance last night while he was jogging. Are you okay? You look awesome! Love that modern medicine!"

My mouth fell open. Everyone started to whisper. I ran into my classroom, hoping no one heard, but they had. Sabrina had a really loud voice.

"You what?" Jimmy asked.

"Uh…" I stumbled.

"When? How?"

"Nng," I stumbled again. I couldn't speak.

"Okay," my teacher announced. "Let's get started. Jimmy, better get to your class, before the second bell."

Lisa was in my class. She passed a note to me. I ignored it.

At recess, Jimmy was waiting for me by my locker.

"I just had a little trouble breathing," I told him, before he could ask me anything.

"A little?"

"Look, it's no big deal. I'm just under a little bit of stress, okay? I'm fine now, as you can see."

He looked stunned.

I took a book out of my locker, sat down on the floor, and began to read.

"Okay. Fine." Jimmy said sadly as he walked away. LAG and David were nowhere in sight, because they were in detention.

* * *

The following night, as I was getting ready to leave for my very first meeting of Frieda's Happy Losers, Lee caught me in the entrance hall and said:

"Have fun at Fatty Club!"

"Hey, it's Frieda's Happy Losers to you, pal."

"Fatty Club," he said.

"At least I'm doing something about it!" I said.

"What about your running shoes? You can do something about it with them."

"Maybe I need to tackle the food issue first, before I go running," I said.

"Suit yourself."

"Lee, please! Support her in this," my mother yelled from the kitchen.

"Okay, fine. It's just that I have a problem with the idea of shelling out money for a stupid eating program that you could follow perfectly well by yourself. All you have to do is cut out the desserts and run outside—for free!"

"Maybe it's easier for you, Mr. Perfect," I yelled back. "I can't do all of that on my own. I need help, okay?"

"No, you don't," he said. His veins were popping out of his forehead.

I took a deep breath and walked out the door with my mother. She was coming with me for support—and to give me a lift, of course.

As soon as we got there, I scanned the room. There must have been at least thirty people in line. I breathed a sigh of relief that the only person I knew was the receptionist from my orthodontist's office. I waved hello.

Finally, it was my turn to get on the scale. First the attendant measured my height. Five foot three. Totally cool with that. Then she weighed me. My eyes popped out of my eye sockets as the dial on the scale kept creeping up and up until it finally balanced. She announced my weight. "Hey, not so loudly!" I shushed. "Oh that's not so bad," she said as she looked at my height and weight and smiled. Let's start with you losing ten pounds for now."

She beamed. She handed me some forms to fill out and a weekly weigh-in booklet. I was all set to go.

With my head to the floor, I walked over to a bunch of chairs arranged in a circle and began to fill out the forms. My mother joined me.

"You'll do great!" mom said.

"Nng," I mumbled.

The chairs in the circle began to fill up. After I was finished, a woman around my mom's age came to the centre of the circle.

"Welcome! I'm Frieda! And welcome to Frieda's Happy Losers!" she squealed. Everyone applauded.

"Let's say hello to some newcomers!" she announced.

No no nooooooooooo, I thought to myself.

"Hello to you!" Frieda said to me, way too happily.

"Hi," I said shyly. I wanted to crawl under my chair.

"You don't seem that overweight, but good for you for coming here before it gets out of hand!" said Frieda.

I nodded. I didn't know if that was appropriate, so I added a smile and a confused look.

"That was embarrassing," a lady beside me said.

I shrugged. That was nothing, I thought, compared to what I've been through that week.

Frieda welcomed a few more people and then lectured us on what to do when you are at a party and there is a buffet full of sweets. Neat idea: Carry a purse in one hand and a Diet Coke in another. No more hands to nosh with.

"Time to take the shoes out of your closet, then," Lee announced one night after dinner.

"Oh, no." I was nervous. I breathed deeply and agreed to go.

As we walked down our steps to the street, my heart began to pound—and I hadn't even started to run yet. Lee began slowly and I followed. When he picked up the pace a little I became lost in his dust, of course. For a while I started to walk because I had a huge cramp in my side. I ignored Lee's yells of frustration as best I could. After a while of this torture, Lee finally stopped jogging and I caught up to him, his hands on his hips and his head bent forward. He was giving me an evil look.

"At least I'm out here, trying!" I said, gasping for air.

"Yeah, I know. Sorry. It's just going to take a while."

As the end of the week neared, I started to get excited about my weigh-in. When the day came, I found out that I'd lost two pounds! Two pounds! I skipped all the way home.

That night as I lay in bed, I imagined how I would look and feel after I lost all the weight that I wanted to lose. Then, I thought about Jimmy. I was so frustrated that I didn't have the guts to talk to him at school, but I sure could think about him at night. I did that very well.

Once in a while I thought about Sam, too, but I thought about Jimmy more. Being with him at Gail's party left an imprint in my mind that kept coming back to me. No one had ever made me feel like that.

Chapter 15

My alarm woke me up from a deep sleep. Once I gained consciousness, I glanced at my bedroom window. It was pitch-black outside, and my eyes frowned at the sight of it. Not surprising for a November morning but not welcomed either. I really didn't like November. It was too cold to hang out outside, and the colourful fall leaves on the ground were all wet and mushy. Most importantly, there was no snow to ski on yet.

I shut my eyes tight and huddled under my warm blanket, in fear of another day of school. I opened my eyes again to look at my clock. It read 6:34 am.

I didn't want to get up.

There was a knock at my door.

It was Lee. "Hey, it's me."

"Hi," I answered.

He went into my closet and came out with my running shoes in his arms.

"I will give you a lift to school this morning if you come running with me for twenty minutes. Just twenty."

"Okay, but no yelling," I said as I threw the covers off my body and grabbed my shoes away from him.

I quickly got dressed and went to meet Lee in the downstairs hallway. As he opened the front door, a strong gust of wind blew onto our bodies. It was cold, but I liked the way it felt.

"Let's go," I said.

I started to jog and Lee was beside me. This time I didn't have to spit saliva from my mouth like a ball player, nor did I feel like an abused animal. All Lee did was jog quietly beside me at a steady slow pace. We jogged around the block four times.

"Okay. That's twenty minutes," said Lee. "Let's go shower."

"Not bad," I said. "I'd do that again."

"Good. So would I." He patted me on the shoulder.

As I undressed in the bathroom, I didn't feel tired; I felt more awake. I was only sweaty around my face and back, and as I showered, I couldn't stop smiling.

I went to school that morning a little more relaxed, but still on edge. I added up my assets: Friends = Zero. Nada. Zilch.

I walked to my locker, and Jimmy was waiting there. This boy did not give up.

"Hi," he said.

I half nodded.

"You know, we should talk about what happened on the intercom, you know, before you were in the hospital and everything." He was smiling. He looked nervous. I was nervous. I mean, I wanted to talk to him, to be with him, to kiss him—but I wanted all the bad stuff to go away: the humiliation, the diary-reading on the intercom, and especially Sabrina Banks and her huge mouth. I wanted to live in a bubble, with Jimmy Singer.

"So," he began.

"So they got detention," I said.

"How do you feel about that?"

"Well, at first I couldn't breathe, as you know, but, well, like I said before, I'm okay now."

He crinkled his eyebrows, like he was confused. Which, by the way, made him look extremely adorable—but thankfully, I did not show any signs of admiration.

Silence.

We both looked at the floor and then at each other. I couldn't take the pressure anymore.

"K—can you just go?" I blurted out.

"Sure. Let me know if you want to talk," he said, looking disappointed.

I nodded.

Talk? Why would I want to talk? What was I supposed to say? The weight on my shoulders was becoming too heavy. It hurt to turn my neck.

Thankfully LAG and David were nowhere in sight. Staying away from me must have been one of the stipulations of their punishment.

The first period bell finally rang. I had math and, even though I didn't understand anything, I didn't care because I had somewhere to go to keep my mind occupied.

I sat in the front row in order not to be disturbed by anyone. I felt the painful stares towards every angle of my body.

"Sorry guys. I had to take a phone call," Mr. Drane said breathlessly as he entered the classroom. He sat his briefcase down at his desk and began his lesson.

I put everything out of my head and tried to concentrate. When the bell rang, I collected my books and started walking towards the door, but Mr. Drane called my name.

"Oh, Lizzie?"

"Yeah?"

"You know, you should come to my math clinic," he said.

"Oh, you have one of those?"

"You bet," he said, with a satisfied look on his face.

"Who else goes?" I asked.

"So far, just me." He smiled.

"So, it would be just you and me?"

"Looks like it."

"Okay. Let me get back to you on that," I said.

"Please do. I'm open, every day, lunch hour."

Second period. Third period. The bell rang for lunch.

I took my tuna sandwich and V8 out of my locker.

I walked into the girls' bathroom, went into a stall, and closed the door. I got up on the tank, placed my feet on the toilet paper holder, and bit into my sandwich. A piece of lettuce fell into the toilet.

Chapter 16

Two weeks later, I came home from school and went straight to my room to plop on my bed. As I lay there, in my famous chilling-out position, I glanced around my room. My eyes stopped on the pile of books that I had just dumped on my desk. They looked really nice there, sitting by themselves, unopened. A lump in my throat told me that before I knew it, exams would be around the corner. I thought I should be a little more organized this year with my studying schedule since my current social life was as exciting as a rice cake.

I shrugged, ignoring that studious idea that sounded so responsible and ambitious. Instead, I opened up my Seventeen magazine and ended up falling asleep on an advertisement for Noxema skin cream.

My drool was all over the model's face, making the magazine page all bumpy and gross. My stomach was grumbling. I glanced at my watch. It was 5:30 and I hadn't even started my homework yet.

"Nng," I said. Of course I had math to do, but I had no idea how to begin. I thought about Mr. Drane's offer to come to his lunchtime "math clinic," and it became more appealing by the minute. What else did I have to do at lunch—become Prom Queen? If I went, I could finally figure out my homework, and I'd have something to do besides eat my lunch on a toilet. Thinking about eating lunch made me think about dinner, and then I thought about Frieda's.

"Oh man!" I yelled. I ran out into the hallway. "My weigh-in is in twenty minutes! Who wants to take me?"

"Yeah, sure," my dad said.

And off we went.

Two pounds down. I beamed all the way home. I loved the way Frieda's was working; it was the only thing in my life that made sense.

It was easy:

Follow the eating plan = Lose weight.

The other situations in my life were not so straight forward.

Read a math question = Get a headache.

Deal with friends = Take a one-way ride on the humiliation train.

Like a guy = See above.

No need to go on.

That night, the phone rang and it was for me. I almost forgot what it was like to speak to someone on the phone.

"Don't hang up!" came Jimmy's voice.

"Okay."

"Look, I know this is hard."

"It is."

"Well, it's hard for me, too." said Jimmy.

"Uh-huh." I said.

"I'm having a hard time concentrating in school."

"Aww, poor baby. Does that mean that you have to switch your math class to my level?" I joked.

"That's not funny." His tone was unpleasant.

I realized my little joke was incredibly stupid. I felt stupid.

"Do you want to talk about it?"

"Not really."

"Why not"

"Just don't want to…look, I gotta go." I hung up the phone. I couldn't find the words to express how I felt and even if I did find the words, I didn't feel like expressing them to anybody.

On most Friday nights, especially during the off ski season, we celebrated Shabbat, the day of rest for us Jews. Since I wasn't that religious, we had a "relaxed" type of Shabbat: It started off with a special dinner that included a few prayers over candles, wine for the adults, grape juice for the kiddies, challah (a braided egg bread), matzoh ball soup, some kind of meat like roasted chicken, potatoes, and an awesome dessert. It is recommended that we say "see ya later" until nighttime on Saturday to anything that deals with work and/or electricity. But in our house, we just ate Shabbat dinner together then went on our separate ways.

During dinner, I did not utter a word. I just sat there and ate: looked up, smiled, and ate until I was full.

Later, I plopped myself on my bed and stared straight ahead, not knowing what to do with myself.

A knock came at the door.

"Yeah?" I said.

"Put on your new jeans. Fix yourself up." It was Lee.

"Why?" I asked.

"Meet me at the front door in twenty minutes."

As Lee and Linda got into the car, I kept asking a million questions. They ignored me and kept raising the volume on the car radio. After a while, I noticed that we were heading downtown and into the McGill ghetto. We parked, Linda handed me some lip gloss, and we headed to an apartment building.

The reggae music was pulsing throughout the hallway, and my heart was beating a mile a minute because I had no idea where I was going or who I was going to meet. Lee opened the door to the party, and the music enveloped us with a loud blaring beat.

There were tons of people in this apartment, scattered everywhere—in the kitchen, in bedrooms, and in the main living area, where there was a small TV and an iPod that was attached to speakers. Right away, some guy saw Lee and informed him that there was a hockey game on in the back bedroom. As fast as Linda could turn around, Lee was gone. She shrugged and smiled at me.

Linda introduced me to a bunch of people, and my eyes darted all around the room. It was amazing. Everyone was smiling, laughing, and looked so relaxed. It was a nice change from the last party I was at. Then, someone handed me a beer.

"Take it," Linda said. I looked at her.

"Take it," she said again, smiling.

"I uh… uh…"

"Come on, midterms are over!" said a girl who was holding a bunch of beers.

"Oh, I'm not in university," I said.

"How old are you?" she asked.

"Fifteen," I said, shyly.

"I could have sworn that you were in my sociology class. You look familiar."

I thought that was so cool. I decided to take the beer. I took a sip and made a sour face.

"Oh, don't worry," said Linda. "I hated it at first too, but then after so many parties, it started to taste pretty good. You'll see."

I couldn't imagine that happening, but then again, my present social life took me by surprise, so who was I to predict the future of my taste buds?

I continued to hold the beer in my hand. I kind of felt silly holding a drink that I didn't like, but I kept holding it because it gave my hands something to do. I took a deep breath and wished that I could skip high school and go to university with Lee.

All of a sudden, we heard a loud, disappointed "Aww." The hockey game was over and a whole bunch of people came into the living room.

"Aw, Lind, you should have seen that missed shot!" Lee said as he hugged Linda.

"Yeah, I really should have," she said sarcastically, her face nuzzled into his armpit.

Lee looked at her and gave her the okay-I-get-it-that-you-don't-like-hockey look. Then he turned to me.

"Having fun, Lizzie?"

I smiled and nodded.

He put his arm around Linda and they walked towards a group of their friends.

"I haven't seen you around campus," came an unfamiliar voice from behind me. I turned around and saw a guy with a beard. I had never been to a party with people with beards before (relatives didn't count). He had big, blue eyes and a nice warm smile that exposed a crooked front tooth.

"Hi," he said, putting out his hand. "John."

"Lizzie," I said, shaking his hand with my free one. I took a sip of my yucky beer and made another sour face.

"Don't like your beer?" he asked.

"Not really."

"Follow me."

I followed him into the kitchen. He went into the fridge and took out a jug of orange juice and poured it into a glass. Then he went into the freezer and took out a bottle of vodka. He poured the vodka into a shot glass, filling it halfway, and then poured that into the orange juice glass.

"Hey, my parents drink that kind," I said.

He added some ice and stirred it with a spoon.

"Now, put down that beer and drink this." He handed me the drink.

I took a small sip.

"Not bad. Pretty good," I said.

"See? You're a cool chick, I can tell. Cool chicks drink screwdrivers."

"Screwdrivers?"

"That's the name, sweetheart. When you have one, just use half a shot of vodka. You don't want to be puking, just happy."

"Okay," I said. I thought this guy was completely cool.

I took some more sips. It was sweet and had a little kick to it. It went down easy.

"So what brings you to this soiree?" he asked.

"Oh… I had three party invites and decided to dump them all and come to this one instead."

"Got into a fight with your friends and your brother felt bad for you so he brought you here?"

My eyes popped out of their sockets.

"Been around… and also Lee told me earlier," John said with a little giggle.

I nodded.

"You know, just a moment ago, a girl thought I was in her sociology class," I announced proudly, hoping to change the subject.

"That girl thinks everybody is in her sociology class…" he laughed.

"Oh," I said.

"…but you could pass for eighteen," he said.

I smiled with all of my teeth showing.

"That thing with your friends… that must have totally sucked," he said.

I looked away.

"I take it that you don't want to talk about it," he said.

I glanced at my screwdriver and took a big gulp. And then another. John came closer to me and put his hand on my shoulder. I kept drinking until it was all gone.

"Can I have another?" I asked.

"No."

"Why?"

"Because cleaning up puke is not my thing," John said.

"Oh. You really don't like vomit, eh?"

"You got it."

"Yeah, neither do I," I said looking down at the floor.

He took my hand and led me to the living room, then motioned for me to sit on a huge beanbag chair.

Then I started talking. I talked about LAG, David spinning me, math, Frieda's Happy Losers, and, of course, Jimmy. John sat there and took it all in, adding comments where necessary.

After a while, Lee and Linda came by our chair and said that it was time for us to go home. As I left and said good-bye to John, I told him that I would always remember my first screwdriver.

Lee and Linda's eyes popped out of their heads.

"Relax guys," said John. "We were sitting here the whole time."

"We were," I confirmed. I felt as if a ton of bricks had been released from my shoulders.

"And you know," John said, addressing my brother, "you don't just leave a high school girl at a party and run off. It's a good thing I'm a decent guy. I could have gotten your sister totally drunk and who knows what else."

"Lizzie can take care of herself," Lee argued.

"Uh, she asked for a second drink and I cut her off," said John.

Lee shrugged defensively.

"But look, bringing her here was a great idea," said John. "It took her mind off of the stupid yahoos who've been treating her like dirt."

I burst out laughing.

"Just keep an eye on her next time."

"Will do," said Lee, embarrassed.

John helped me put on my coat. "You know what you have to do, Lizzie?" he asked.

"Besides the no puking at parties? Not really."

"You will."

Chapter 17

On Monday morning, I woke up a few minutes before my alarm went off. I breathed deeply and headed to the bathroom. I stepped into the shower stall and smiled as the warm water covered my body like a blanket. I thought about my weekend and what a great time I had at the McGill party in the ghetto.

Lisa, Amanda, and Gail would think it was so totally cool that I'd gone to that party and spent time with a really great guy named John who was smart and funny and had a beard. I'd spent an entire evening with bearded John, who told me not to drink beer but to drink a screwdriver with fancy vodka. Most importantly, level-headed, bearded John—unlike all the other adults in my life—hadn't told me to go empty the dishwasher, or pick up my clothes from the floor, or do my homework.

I thought about forgiving LAG. Maybe they had been punished enough. Their detention was officially over, and I decided that it would be a great idea to start fresh. As I lathered my hair with shampoo, I started to smile and get excited about running up to Lisa and telling her how much I hated beer and that screwdrivers with the right kind of vodka were so cool. Then I would run up to Gail and tell her how much I liked the music, and then I would tell Amanda about John and all the other cute guys that were there.

I got dressed, slathered on some gel on my hair and put on a little bit of blush and mascara, then I walked quickly to the kitchen to eat my breakfast. I almost choked from eating too quickly.

"Why the rush?" my mom asked as she handed me some orange juice.

"Oh, I've go things to do," I said.

"Don't forget to…" yelled my mother, the dentist.

"I'm gonna right now!" I yelled from the hallway as I ran to the bathroom.

I darted to the bathroom to brush my teeth (G-d forbid I should let my breakfast sit on my teeth for the whole day). I smoothed on some lip gloss, grabbed my iPod, and dashed out the door.

As I approached my locker, I noticed that something smelled like garbage and lo and behold, my bright, shiny bubble of enthusiasm burst.

I opened my locker and a whole bunch of rotten food fell out. Black bananas, apple cores, and chocolate pudding cups. I stood there, speechless, while out of the corner of my eye I saw Amanda standing there, smiling. My plan of sharing my weekend with her fell to the floor like a raw egg.

I picked up the garbage. My hands were shaking, and it was all I could do to keep from crying. Amanda slithered up to me.

"Miss your food since you've been at Frieda's?" she asked snidely. "My cousin saw you there. She even saw how much you weighed!"

"That's impossible," I said between clenched teeth. "The scale is in a private place."

"Oh, she saw."

I felt as if Amanda had kicked me right in the stomach. I stood there, staring at her.

"Why?" I asked.

"Why what?" she asked.

"Why do you keep torturing me?"

"Oh come on, it's funny!"

"Rotten food in a locker is not funny. Spreading gossip about how much I weigh is not funny, and stealing my diary and reading it into the intercom is not fucking funny either!"

I slammed my locker shut and went to the bathroom to splash my face with cold water. Of course, Lisa and Amanda were by the sinks. They stopped talking in mid-sentence when they noticed me.

"So, you guys into using my locker as a garbage dump, too?" I asked, seething.

"Amanda did it," Gail said.

"I know who did it, moron," I said.

"So why are you asking us?" Gail asked.

"Because the three of you work together."

"I'm really sorry about that," Lisa said sheepishly.

"Yeah, right."

I heard footsteps behind me. I turned around and it was Amanda.

"What's all the commotion here?" Amanda asked, smiling.

"It's nothing," Lisa said nervously.

"Yeah, she's just washing her hands," Gail said.

Washing my hands of my so-called friends, I thought to myself.

I shouted, "Why are you still treating me like a punching bag? Didn't you already have enough? Didn't you learn anything from detention?"

The three of them just stared at me. I walked out of the bathroom.

As I walked with loud stomps towards my locker, two girls stopped me.

"We heard everything that went on in the bathroom!" said one.

"Yeah," said the other. "They think they're such hot stuff!"

"Yeah," said the first one. "Why don't you hang out with us?"

"Uh, thanks guys." I smiled and looked down at them. They were very sweet, very cute seventh-graders. I patted them both on the shoulder and continued walking.

As for the rest of the kids in my grade, most of them avoided LAG. They also avoided me because they didn't want to get involved with the whole mess. I still couldn't believe that just a few months ago we had been so inseparable—and then out of nowhere, I was alone.

When I got home that afternoon, Lee was packing for a hockey game. "What's with the new hockey bag?" I asked, noticing the shiny new exterior of the bag and the tags on the floor.

"Last one had too many holes. Smelled gross," he explained.

"Oh," I said softly.

"What's wrong?" He turned and noticed my tear-filled eyes.

"Oh, LAG put some garbage in my locker today. Gave me a hard time," I confessed.

"What do you mean garbage?" he asked, confused.

"Garbage. You know, banana peels, pudding cups?"

"Wha?"

"Yup."

For about five minutes, Lee went off on a swearing fiesta. He only swore like that when he was pissed. I guess he was really pissed.

When Dad got home he brought me a basket of fresh berries. He even made a smoothie for me, and it was delicious. At least I'm loved at home, I thought, as I slurped the last sip from my glass.

* * *

Later that week, my parents informed Lee and me that this year, during our Christmas break, it was our family's turn to visit Grandma L and Grandpa B (Lillian and Bill, respectively; Dad's parents) at their Florida condo.

My grandparents owned a really nice apartment at the beach that was a part of a retirement community. There was a clubhouse along with a few restaurants, tennis courts, and a movie theatre. Everywhere you looked, there were three-wheel bicycles being pedalled by grandmas, and crowds of white-haired people speed-walking along a walking trail.

The apartment was made for a couple plus one family to come and visit. One year, the extended family—six cousins, two aunts, and two uncles—had decided that we could all visit at the same time during Christmas break. What a nightmare that was! I slept on the floor in a homemade sleeping bag, and I vowed never to do it again. Sharing one bathroom with seven other kids and six adults was just not cool—especially after Uncle Steven used the toilet.

That year, only the four of us were going, which would make things much less squishy and much more comforting. Even though it was fun being with the entire family all at once, I needed to have some quiet time with my immediate family and my grandparents. That vacation was a month away and I wanted to leave. Now.

But exams were three weeks away and I had to get cracking. Since my social life was extremely busy—NOT—I stuck to my studies like a worm to mud. And from time to time, I daydreamed about how my feet would feel sinking into the warm soft sand on the beach—and, of course, what Jimmy was up to, but I didn't tell anyone that.

The next week, during lunch, as I was headed towards my bathroom stall, I decided to take a turn and go somewhere else. With my lunch bag in hand, I knocked on the door.

"Come in," said Mr. Drane.

Chapter 18

Standing in front of the closed door, I clutched my books to my chest.

"Come in!" I heard Mr. Drane say for the second time. I kept standing there.

"Hello?" he said again.

I took a deep breath and opened the door. Mr. Drane was a man in his mid-forties. He had salt-and-pepper hair (with more salt than pepper), was not too skinny and not too fat, and he didn't have that "old man stomach" that a lot of my friends' dads had. This must have been due to his daily jogs every morning. How did I know that he jogged? Sometimes during math class, he would stop in mid-sentence and say, "Geez, I'm tight. I didn't stretch today after my run." He had a goatee that was mysteriously darker than the hair on his head, and wore reading glasses that he only used when marking tests. Mr. Drane took his wardrobe up a notch by wearing a suit while the other male teachers only wore a shirt and tie.

I walked slowly into the classroom.

"I don't bite," he said, smiling.

"I know," I felt shy.

He was holding a stainless-steel cup filled with coffee, and there was a sandwich on his desk, surrounded by tin foil. I could smell it from where I was standing. Fresh roast beef on rye. As my mouth began to water, I made a mental note for myself to make sure my parents bought roast beef the next time they went shopping.

"Glad you're here," he said, taking a bite of his sandwich.

"Oh, yeah, well, I figured I'd give it a try. I mean, I've got nothing better to do."

"Thanks a lot," said Mr. Drane.

"Oh, I didn't mean that." I was so embarrassed.

"Then what did you mean?" he asked. He crossed his arms in mock indignation.

"It's just that…well…"

"You didn't have anything better to do," he laughed.

"I guess."

"Look, it's alright. I have a hard time believing it myself—that not everyone likes me."

My eyes widened with interest. "Some people do," I said hopefully.

"Just like the dentist," he said.

"My parents are dentists," I laughed.

"Aha! And you like them, right?"

"Most of the time," I joked.

"Did you eat?" he asked.

"Oh yeah, I just wolfed down a tuna on a kaiser roll."

"Oh yes, the tuna on a kaiser, my second favourite. I usually get that on Fridays."

"Why on Fridays?" I asked.

"I let my kids make it for me. I don't start until second period on Fridays so I have more time. They like to use the can opener, add a little mayo, squeeze a little lemon, and add some spinach for crunch and iron." He sounded proud.

"How old are your kids?" I asked.

"Sasha is ten, and Ben is eight."

"Nice," I said.

"Yeah," he said, but very quietly, and seemed to trail off.

I was confused, and looked at him.

"I just think of Jeff sometimes." His voice had dropped; he sounded sad.

"Who's Jeff?"

"My son who died."

I felt my face fall to the floor.

"Car accident. He was thirteen." He spoke just above a whisper.

"Oh, my G-d. When did this happen?" I asked. I felt my body shaking.

"Four years ago."

"He would be seventeen now," I said.

"Hey, the girl can add!"

I was taken aback, but I smiled.

"That was a joke," he said.

"I know. I didn't find it funny," I said.

"Do you drink coffee?" he asked, obviously ready to change the topic. I had been wondering when we would start some math. But I didn't want to say anything because, as bad as it sounded, I preferred anything—even our morbid conversation—to math.

"Coffee? Excuse me?" I was confused.

"You know, the black stuff your parents brew every morning."

"Not really," I said.

"Well, you should try my roast. Here, it's decaf." He poured some coffee from his thermos into an extra cup from his desk. I took the cup and sipped. It was delicious. It tasted like warm coffee ice cream.

"Wow," I said.

"Good, huh?"

"My parents always have coffee brewing in the morning. It smells good, but I just think people talk about coffee too much."

"Oh, I know." He looked amused.

The bell rang.

"Great math tutoring," I said.

"There's always tomorrow."

"Oh yes, tomorrow. Let me check my social calendar." I was becoming a master of sarcasm.

"This is the better thing to do tomorrow," he said.

* * *

When I got home that afternoon, I plopped on my bed and maneuvered into my chilling-out position. I thought again about Mr. Drane's late son Jeff and it made me feel sick to my stomach. I couldn't imagine what that was like. What he had to face every day—like seeing Jeff's old friends grow up—and just living every day without him. My troubles seemed worthless compared to that, and I felt guilty for complaining about them.

I glanced at the bulletin board that held my calendar. It was the last week of November and I had two weeks until exams started. Since I was in no mood for math (big surprise there), I decided to crack open the French and home economics, two things that seemed doable to me.

* * *

The next day, when the lunch bell rang, I officially decided to stop eating on a toilet flusher and walk directly to Mr. Drane's math class. With lunch bag in one hand and books in the other, I knocked on the door.

"Come on in!" he called cheerfully.

"Thanks!" I said as entered the classroom. I walked up to his desk, planted my lunch bag on his desk, grabbed a chair, and sat down to eat. I took a huge bite of my turkey sandwich. My mother hadn't gone shopping yet for the roast beef, so turkey was the next best thing.

"Lizzie, I didn't mean to dump that information about my son Jeff's death on you yesterday."

While chewing, I nodded.

"I really don't talk about him much," he continued. I was still chewing.

"I guess it just came out, and I'm sorry if it made you feel uncomfortable."

I finally swallowed. "It's okay; it's life," I said.

"Yes, it's full of surprises," he said.

"You don't have to tell me that."

"Right," he smiled. "So, since we didn't get a chance to do any math yesterday, why don't you tell me what you want to work on today, and that's where we'll start."

I took another bite of my sandwich and thought about it. "Slopes," I said finally. "I hate them."

"Well, let's tackle that mountain... math humour," Mr. Drane joked. And we tackled it. By the time the lunch bell rang, I was swooshing through the slopes a little more easily.

* * *

On the Sunday night, one week before December exams started, I was in the kitchen making myself dinner. As I scrambled my eggs, I thought about my past week. No one had bothered me, and I had spent every afternoon at Mr. Drane's math class going over stuff. While working on the equations, my shoulders didn't seem to rise to my earlobes like they used to, and I was beginning to go over the work on my own at home. I felt good, but still lonely and still angry.

The next morning, a huge snow storm fell on the city. All the schools were closed and most businesses were too, including my parents' dental office. The four of us were home together, and that was when the second storm hit.

I was in the kitchen drinking my new favourite drink. It was early, just after the news informed us that everything would be closed. Lee came in, scratching his head, still wearing his pajamas.

"Since when do you drink coffee?" he asked.

"Since recently."

"Not exactly the best thing for you," he said, pouring his orange juice.

"Yeah, I know. But I don't drink Coke. It's decaf.

"Fine. One cup a day. No more."

"Fine, Mon Capitan!" I saluted.

"Speaking of fattening, how is Fatty Club going?" he asked.

"Great. Lost two pounds this week." I said.

"Not bad."

"Thanks."

My mother walked in.

"That would be six pounds in total." I said.

"That's great, sweetie!" my mother gushed. Lee left the room. My mother stopped at the counter and made a worried face.

"What's wrong?" I asked.

"There's something I need you to do." she said.

"Okay."

"I want you to start seeing a therapist when we get home from Florida."

"No way," I said.

"Why not?"

"Because."

I got up from the table and started to pace back and forth.

"Because why?" she asked after a pause.

"I don't need to. I'm fine."

"Yes you do, and no you are not." She was firm.

"Who said?" I yelled.

"I did, and I am your mother." I could tell she was losing her patience. "And I said so."

She walked over to the table and motioned for me to sit down with her. I did and held my cup of coffee. She looked at my coffee mug and made a confused face.

"Yes, I like coffee now. It's decaf," I said.

"What are you afraid of?" she asked.

I shrugged.

"You can't do this all alone," she whispered.

"I have Jenny," I said.

"Jenny, who does not go to your school and who travels all over the country for recitals?"

I looked at my coffee cup.

"How did you find this therapist?" I asked.

"She's my patient."

"Eew. Ma," I whined. "Do you tell all of your patients about me?"

"It's not like that. I knew what she did for a living and she is a lovely woman. I could really see you connecting with her."

"Who is she?" I asked.

"Her name is Marna."

* * *

For the rest of the snow day, I stayed in my pajamas. I checked my email, which included nothing except for an announcement about a sale at the mall. In my room, I did some homework and did not come out until my stomach was growling for lunch. On the way to the kitchen, I met Lee in the hallway. He informed me that I was going with him for a run in the snow after lunch.

"Do I even have a choice?" I asked.

"Nope." he laughed.

I had to digest my meal and finish up my studying, so when we finally went, it was 3:00 pm. We dressed in our ski outfits so we wouldn't get wet.

A run in the snow turned out to be more like swimming in the snow. Every time we tried to run, we would fall on our faces. The sidewalks on our street were not cleared yet, so it was impossible to run.

Lee kept yelling at himself. "Come on! Why can't I run?" He hollered as he fell on his face.

It was too funny watching him get mad at snow.

Once we got to the park, we made snow angels and ran and fell and ran and fell and ran again. We both could not stop laughing. When we'd had enough, we walked home. We found a snow removal truck heading to our street and walked behind it. When we got home, my dad made us hot chocolate. I felt like I was six, but I didn't care.

The next day, school was open, and as boring as it seemed, I welcomed the monotony with open arms. With my life being a roller coaster of emotions, I threw myself into a studying routine.

I should have known that temptation would finally arise; that day, it did. There it was: A huge gift basket that my parents received from one of their patients. Besides the bottle of wine, fancy cheese and crackers and fruit, there, in the middle, lay my one and only love of my life: an enormous bag of M&M's. My eyes popped out like popcorn kernels when I saw that beautiful shiny brown bag with the colourful logo. The basket sat on our kitchen counter, staring at me. Every time I passed by, I could have sworn I could smell the chocolate through the cellophane wrapping and huge gold bow.

"Say, why don't we bring the basket over to Connie and David's tomorrow night? It will liven up the game." My dad was referring to my parents' poker night at their friend's house.

"Eew, that's gift recycling!" my mom said, screwing up her nose.

Yes! Yes! Take it! Take it away! I yelled in my head.

"Yeah…I guess so. You never know who'll be there," my dad said.

"I guess we could keep it," said my mom.

No! No! Get it out of the house! I was screaming so loudly in my head, I think my earrings were rattling.

"Lee," my mom asked, "would you like to take the bottle of wine over to Linda's house?"

"Yeah, sure."

My brother looked over and saw me staring at the basket, drooling. "And the M&M's. I'll take them, too," he said.

I breathed a sigh of relief.

After dinner, as I was doing the dishes, I kept staring at the basket. I felt my mouth salivating.

Lee walked into the kitchen.

I cut my finger on a knife. "Ouch!" I yelled.

"That's what happens when you're hypnotized."

"Is it that obvious?"

"Oh, just have one. Go on. Take a bunch."

I couldn't help it. Here was my trainer, giving me permission to devour my favourite treat. I dried my hands on a nearby towel and ripped off the cellophane wrapper like a bear invading a camper's food stash. I opened up the huge bag of M&M's with such force, the bag split in two and the M&M's were all over the floor, but I didn't care. I bent down and grabbed as many as I could and shoved them into my mouth. I chewed the chocolate bits quickly, allowing them to melt and slide down my throat while I felt the rush of pleasure run through my body. I took another bunch into my mouth and gave out a whimper of delight. Lee looked at me and frowned.

"Go ahead, take another handful." he said.

And I did. And then suddenly, I stopped chewing. It didn't taste the same. It turned bland. Almost tasteless. I spit the last bite out into the sink.

"Wow." I said.

Lee nodded and smiled.

I went to Fatty Club the next evening to be weighed. Miraculously, I'd lost a pound.

Two handfuls of M&M's hadn't broken the bank. And the fact that I stopped after two made me feel like I had beaten the beast. I finally felt that the M&M's no longer controlled me.

I wrote my exams feeling a little more at ease because I had found a missing piece of one of my life's puzzle.

Chapter 19

The plane trip to Florida was one long sardine-in-a-can ride. I really hated that I had to climb over three people's laps in order to go to the bathroom and the fact that I had to wave frantically to the stewardess walking by just to alert her that I needed water. Dry airplane air made me thirsty! She of course pretended that she didn't see me when I damn well knew that my long arms waving were in full view.

"Like you didn't see me. Puh-lease!" I said. Other passengers giggled.

I crossed my tired arms over my chest and sank into my chair. My throat was dry. I daydreamed of the beautiful soothing ocean and the way my feet would sink into the warm, silky sand.

I thought about my last week of school. No frown, no smile—just blah. I had been alone all week, I had written my exams—and who knows how I'd done on them. I had spent almost two full weeks of lunch hours in Mr. Drane's class. We had worked hard—or, at least, I had worked hard. So hard that every time I left his classroom, I left with a headache.

One day we exchanged half of our sandwiches, and another I had a cup of coffee that Mr. Drane called "sweet and smooth." As I held the warm Styrofoam cup in my hand, he pointed out all the different flavoured notes the coffee contained.

"Oh, gimme a break. It's just coffee!"

"Patience, patience. You'll get it." he promised, like a wise old sage.

One day, we talked about Jeff. Mr. Drane had just finished drawing a diagram on the chalkboard when he gave me a funny look.

"What is it?" I asked nervously.

"Your face—it reminded me of Jeff. He did the same thing with his eyebrows whenever he was confused about something. You lifted your right eyebrow. Just like him."

"It's a rare talent." I said, lightening the moment.

During my exam, Mr. Drane had come up to my desk and given me a how's-it-going-I-know-you-can-do-this look. I had smiled and hoped that what I was writing down would add up.

I returned to the present moment from thinking about my last week of school because I had to go to the bathroom. I jumped over three laps and marched to the back of the plane. My eyes nearly popped out of my head when I saw him, sitting and reading a novel.

I couldn't believe it: how could Jimmy Singer be on my plane? I kept on walking, looking straight ahead like the stewardess. I didn't think he saw me. Miraculously, there was no line-up, so I quickly peed, washed my hands, and fixed my hair—because due to the airplane climate, I looked like an electrical experiment. I splashed on some water, which made my hair worse. "Ugh!" I said to my reflection. I gave up and left the bathroom to make my way back to my seat.

Of course, our eyes met.

"Hello." I said shyly.

"Hey—what are the chances?" he said.

"Okay," I said. "See ya."

It was all I could manage. I rushed back to my seat, sat down, and took a deep breath. Lee, who was sitting next to me with a worried expression, said, "You look like you saw a ghost."

"Oh no, no ghost. Just Jimmy Singer."

"Oh." Lee smiled.

"You know, I saw him at the ticket counter, but I didn't want to upset you."

"Upset me?" I whispered loudly. "At least I could have been a little prepared!"

"How did I know he was going to be on our plane? Hundreds of planes fly every day."

"Oh, shut up. It's too late now." I was breathing heavily.

Five minutes later, Jimmy came up to my seat and I was trapped in another conversation with him.

"Watcha reading?" he asked.

"Oh, a trashy novel."

"Any good?"

"Oh yeah," I said. "It's hot."

I felt like such a moron.

Lee butted in and asked Jimmy if he played hockey. *Great!* I'm off the hook for having to talk to a guy that I have been avoiding for the past two months. Because really, what do you say to a guy that you have been dragged through the complete humiliation train with?

For the next five minutes, both guys were talking about Lee's favourite sport, and it put my mind at ease enough that I was able to think of what else to say.

Jimmy turned to me.

"Do you play hockey, Lizzie?"

Lee laughed.

"Excuse me…" I glowered at Lee. "No, but I ski." I said proudly.

"Nice."

I smiled and nodded.

"How was your vectors exam?" I quickly asked, not wanting to nod and smile anymore.

"Oh, it was cool."

"Cool?" I said.

"I remembered when I took that course, man, what a blast!" Lee laughed.

A blast? I smiled at these two, the weirdest guys on the plane. The weirdest guys in the world.

I then came out with another fantastic question: "Where are you staying?" And when he told me, I nearly flew off my chair! This was all too much of an insane coincidence. He was staying in the building next to my grandparents! His family shared an apartment with another family, and it was his turn to come this year as well. I couldn't believe my luck—but I wasn't sure if it was good or bad.

"Oh, great," I said. "Fun!"

I sounded ½ happy, ½ nervous, and ½ sarcastic all at the same time.

Jimmy then announced that he wanted to start a movie before we landed. I nodded and smiled while he spun around and walked back to his seat. I just sat there, still in shock about my vacation neighbour.

I put my headset on and watched a movie, too.

While the opening credits rolled, I decided that it was too much for me to look at Jimmy in the face and carry on a proper conversation without getting sweaty palms and feeling like an idiot. I wondered what he felt about talking to me.

"He totally digs you." said Lee, lifting my headset off my ear.

I crossed my arms over my chest again and sunk into my chair, not paying much attention to the movie.

* * *

When we arrived at the apartment, Grandma L and Grandpa B were excited to have us there.

"Gib a kick," my grandmother squealed. "Zit is ze shayna medelah and medel!"

I translated in my head: "Take a look at these beautiful faces!"

"Lillian, leave them alone!" Grandpa hollered.

I hauled my suitcase to the study/computer room and started to organize my clothes on the floor, since it was going to be my bedroom. It was a small room with a pull-out couch and a desk that held a TV, a computer, and fax machine. I was ecstatic about the TV in my bedroom!

As I sat on the couch, I stared at my reflection in the mirrored closet door and was starting to like the shrinkage that was going on, but I knew that I was not done yet.

I decided to look up Fatty Club in Florida. I checked the yellow pages, and there was a weigh-in centre just three miles from the condo.

Weigh-in was next week, so I was all set to head out to the Dairy Queen to get a Blizzard—so I could get my "last licks." There was one just around the corner. But Lee stopped me.

"Where are you going?"

"To get a Blizzard at Dairy Queen."

"Didn't you learn a lesson from the M&M's last week?"

"I'm not going to have ten of them, just one."

"But why?"

"All I want is one Blizzard. What's the big deal?"

"You're getting ice cream to deal with seeing Jimmy."

"Excuse me?"

"You're not deaf."

He grabbed my running shoes, a pair of shorts, and a T-shirt from my pile of clothes on the floor then threw them at me.

"Get changed. We're going for a run. Don't worry; I'm not a monster."

"Well, you sure sound like one!" I cried.

"I just want you to see how exercise can release tension better than ice cream."

I grunted while I tied up my shoes.

"If you want something cold after our run, we'll go and get something healthy like frozen yogurt, okay?"

First we ran around the village. The place was packed with visitors from all over the place. There were many young families pushing baby carriages and people of all ages puttering around the grounds. After a while of saying "excuse me" at least a thousand times on the walking trail, we decided to move to the beach where we were free to run without anyone around us. The whole ordeal wasn't as bad as I had expected, because Lee was a mile ahead of me, and I couldn't hear his yelling— although I did see him flap his arms up and down, signaling for me to run faster. What had happened to the nice, calm brother of mine from November? In any case, I ignored him and ran at my own pace. At the end of our run, we stopped for frozen yogurt, like he had promised. Funny thing was, I didn't want the Blizzard anymore. The yogurt did the trick. The bastard was right.

* * *

The next day, I brought my trashy book to the pool with me. My parents usually hated it when I read novels like that, but this time, I didn't hear a peep out of them. I guess they were giving me a break because they wanted me to relax. After a while, I decided to put on my iPod and go for a walk. It was on full-blast, and I didn't hear much but the blaring sound of my music.

Suddenly someone tapped me on the shoulder. I turned around and there he was. I knew it was just a matter of time until I bumped into him.

"Oh, hi!" I said. He flashed me his killer smile—the one that made my knees melt.

"Hi." said Jimmy.

"Hi." I said again as I took off my earphones and turned off my iPod.

"Great weather, eh?" he asked.

"Yeah, nice change from Montreal."

"Yeah. I like change. Change is good."

"Very good."

"Yeah."

I smiled, but I was freaking out because I had nothing to say, and I really wanted to continue on my walk.

"Going for a walk?" he said, motioning a speed-walk.

"Yeah, I got some great music here," I said, pointing to my iPod.

"Great."

I had to end the conversation. I was getting antsy and wanted to start walking.

"Okay. Great. See you later," I offered.

"Okay, bye," said Jimmy.

I smiled a really toothy, wide smile and put on my headphones.

As I walked away, I thought about two things: how painfully awkward that whole scene had been and how hot he had looked in his bathing suit. I was sure I had turned three shades of red—that I hoped to pass off as sunburn—during our short but uncomfortable conversation.

I turned back to see where he was. He was still standing there, in the same spot where I'd left him, staring at the ocean. After a couple more songs, I turned around again and he was gone.

Chapter 20

That Friday night, my grandmother was not in the mood to cook Shabbat dinner, so we decided to go to the clubhouse for dinner.

"But we have to light the candles before we go."

"In the sink," my grandfather added.

I looked confused. I knew I was doing the one-eyebrow thing and thought of Mr. Drane's son, Jeff.

"Don't give me that confused look, Lizzie!" my grandfather said. "Would you like to come home to a burnt-to-a-crisp condominium?"

As we lit the candles next to the Palmolive dishwashing detergent, I looked over to see my grandparents. They had huge smiles on their faces.

Along with my mother and grandmother, I said the Friday night prayer on the Shabbat candles. To my surprise, it felt good doing that ritual — peaceful and safe. Afterwards, my grandfather privately gave me a card. Inside, it read:

Roses are red. Violets are blue.
Sometimes a sadness is new.

It isn't bad, just a little scary.

But don't worry; you're my little fairy.

As corny as it was, I couldn't help but smile. As we walked into the clubhouse to be seated, my grandfather waved a torn piece of newspaper in the air like a lottery ticket.

"Look what I have!" he sang.

"Oh my G-d." my dad said when he saw the coupon in his father's hand.

"Hey, a free dessert is a free dessert!" said my grandfather. My dad shook his head in frustration.

I scanned the restaurant, and spotted Jimmy and his family by the waterfall near the entrance door. Without realizing it, I was smiling.

"What are you so happy about?" Lee said to me suspiciously.

"Me? Oh, nothing." I replied, fully lying.

When he walked towards me to get in line for dinner, I ended up giggling out of pure excitement and nervousness. I said hello to his parents and his brother.

"What's so funny?" he asked.

"Oh. My dad cracked a joke. Something about a coupon for dessert."

My dad smiled. I was thrilled that I had thought of something so fast.

Jimmy pointed to his grandmother's hands.

"Same coupon." he said.

"It must be a Florida-grandparent thing."

"Must be."

Just as I was going to introduce Jimmy to my parents, my dad spotted Jimmy's dad and before I knew it they'd made a date to play golf. Then my mother discovered that she used to practice yoga with Jimmy's mother before she was married. Both sets of parents became buddy-buddy, chatting up a storm, and Jimmy and I were standing there in the middle of all the noise. I stood there motionless, smiling off and on, and poor Jimmy was trying to make conversation with me. Lee just stood there enjoying the whole scene, laughing to himself.

"Wanna play paddleball tomorrow on the beach?" Jimmy asked.

"Sure," I answered before I could think about it.

"My brother and I play all the time, but tomorrow he's playing tennis," he said.

Then the restaurant hostess motioned for my family to take our seats.

"Okay," I said. "See ya."

"At about ten?" he said.

"Sure. I'll be by the pool."

I was too excited to eat my dinner.

The next morning, I wore my new bathing suit and didn't wear shorts over it, like I used to wear to cover up my thighs. I wore a long tank top, instead.

I went down to the pool at 9:30 so I could catch some rays before it got too hot. I laid on a chaise lounge, wearing sunglasses and my iPod.

Then I felt a presence. I opened my eyes and took off my sunglasses. I glanced at the figure blocking my sun.

"I am not going for a run now, Lee." I said.

"Okay, fine. But later you will."

"Maybe."

Jimmy showed up and joined Lee, shadowing my body.

137

"I'm going to kick her ass in paddleball," Jimmy said proudly.

"You are not," I argued.

"Go to it," said Lee.

"You're going down," I told Jimmy teasingly.

"It's a good thing your ass is getting smaller," Lee said to me.

I gave him a look that would burn a hole through his body. I wanted to kill him. I was so embarrassed.

But then it was just Jimmy and I, and we were off to the beach.

As I was wrapping my hair in a ponytail holder, I felt Jimmy look at me, but I didn't look back. I was too busy concentrating on the shaggy monster that I call my hair. It was no match for the ocean air, which made it twice its normal size because of the humidity. Where was Lisa and her magic straightening iron?

Jimmy and I began to volley.

Tip tap.

Tip tap.

Tip tap.

Several thoughts ran through my head as we played: this was my first official date with Jimmy, and I hadn't even straightened my hair—it was in a scrunchie. Yeesh. And I hadn't even showered. Double yeesh.

Not much conversation needed during paddle ball. Very good.

I wondered if he was nervous. I was.

Plunk.

Tip tap.

Tip tap.

Tip tap.

"Hey."

"Look at us."

"Wow."

Tip tap.

Tip tap.

"A record."

Plunk.

"Spoke too soon."

Tip tap.

Tip tap.

Tip tap.

"Woo hoo!"

Tip tap.

Tip tap.

This went on for a while, until my shoulders started to burn, my arms felt sore, and I was sick of picking up the ball every time it went "plunk."

"Let's go for a dip." I said. "I'm boiling."

We both dove in. I welcomed the cold water like eating ice cream on a hot summer day. An "ahh" came out of my mouth without realizing it.

"Watcha doin' later?" I asked Jimmy. I couldn't believe those words flew out of my mouth. *Did I just ask him out?*

"I gotta go shopping for a suit. It's my cousin's bar mitzvah next week, here in Florida. That's one of the reasons we came this year." he said.

"Lucky it was your turn for the condo."

"Yeah, everyone else in my family had to dish out cash for a hotel," he joked.

Then he asked, "Want to play again tomorrow?"

"Sure," I said.

He swam up to me, gave me a kiss on the cheek, and left. I remained in the pool, treading, watching him dry off and walk away.

Chapter 21

Lee woke me up the next morning. I don't know what time it was, but it must have been early because the sun wasn't completely up.

He stood over my bed holding a glass of orange juice in one hand and my running shoes in the other.

"I'm already playing paddleball with Jimmy this morning," I said with one eye shut.

"Oh, well, that'll do, I guess," he said and walked towards the door.

"But I can always do both," I said, surprised by what had just come out of my mouth, which was becoming a habit of mine.

"Sure you can," Lee said, smiling.

So we went. I jogged at my steady and slow pace, and Lee was ten miles ahead of me. I didn't care. I was outside, enjoying the beautiful weather and loving the fact that I no longer viewed running as torture.

After we finished the three-mile route around the grounds, we grabbed some lemonade at the coffee shop. I couldn't stop smiling from the euphoria of my run, but I was starving. I couldn't wait to dig into breakfast, and thankfully, when we arrived back at the apartment, a cottage cheese and mushroom omelette with toast was waiting for me.

After breakfast, I brushed my teeth and changed into my bathing suit, then ran down to the beach to meet Jimmy.

Tip tap.

Tip tap.

"You've got Ms. Green for English?" he asked.

"Yeah," I said. "She's so awesome."

"You like her?"

"What's not to like?"

"She's the only one who gave me a lousy B," he complained. "It totally ruined my average."

"A 'B'? Horrors!" I said sarcastically.

"Oh, shut up!" he joked.

Tip tap.

Tip tap.

Tip tap.

"Wanna go for a swim?" he asked.

"I'll race you!"

We ran towards the pool. I was ahead of him at first, and then he was right on my tail, but I picked up the pace and sprinted as fast as I could, which was hard in the soft, silky sand. Then he planted his hand on my shoulder and whizzed passed me.

"Excuuuuse me!" he yelled.

"Hey, ladies first!" I yelled back.

"You wish!" he yelled from the edge of the pool. He jumped in. I jumped in after him, and when his face surfaced, I splashed him.

"Hog!" I joked.

"I know, I wasn't very nice. I really wanted to get into the pool," he offered. "I was hot, what can I say?"

"Whatever. You're still a hog."

"How can I make it up to you?" he asked.

"Hmm," I said. "Come to think of it, I have some shoes that need shining."

"How about after I shine your shoes, I take you to a movie. The new Tom Cruise one."

My eyes widened. "Tonight?" I asked.

He smiled. "Yup."

"But you don't drive," I said.

"But my brother does, and he's going with his girlfriend, who's in town."

I nodded and smiled.

"Great! Pick you up at seven. Gotta go and meet my parental units," He said, and he swam away.

"Apartment 507!" I called after him.

He stepped out of the pool and I was left alone, treading water, coming to terms with the fact that I had a real date with Jimmy. Not just a daytime beach date, but a real date at night with a car and everything. I swam to the side of the pool.

"What am I going to wear?" I caught myself saying aloud.

I decided to put that thought out of my mind until I had to get ready. I wanted to spend the next couple of hours with my nose in my trashy book on the couch.

After an hour, my stomach started to growl. My stomach told my head that I wanted lunch, but my heart wanted to figure out what I was going to wear. I went to the apartment and no one was home. There was a note taped to the fridge.

"Lizzie, enjoy the leftover tuna salad. We went golfing. Love, Mom and Dad."

Okay, great, but what was I going to wear?

I sat down at the table and ate the tuna salad on rye bread with a glass of milk. I glanced at the clock on the stove. It was 2:05 pm. I had 4 hours and 55 minutes to get ready for this date, and I had no idea what I was going to wear.

As I was putting my dishes into the dishwasher, the front door opened.

"What do I wear?" was all I could say to greet my dad.

"Wear to what, sweetheart?"

"I have a date with Jimmy, and I have no idea what to wear."

"Wear clothes, of course," he deadpanned.

"You just don't get it!"

My dad's eyebrows went all scrunchy, and I realized that I'd inherited that trait from him. "So that's what my eyebrows do when I'm in Mr. Drane's math class," I said.

"Excuse me?"

"Oh never mind."

My dad shrugged, but then came the inevitable load of questions:

"Where are you going? How are you getting there? When will you be home? And why are you getting all huffed up about what you'll be wearing?"

"To a movie. With his brother and his brother's girlfriend. At 10:00.

And finally: I guess because this is my first real date with him since we were both humiliated two months ago." I said, and caught my breath.

"Oh, okay," said my dad. "Go have fun then."

"Thanks."

I went to my room to lie down. This was all too much for me. I sat on the couch and stared at my pile of clothes. I pulled out a pair of jeans, a T-shirt, and a bright-blue cardigan to tie around my shoulders in case it got cold in the theatre. I looked at my watch and it read 2:45 pm. I had too much time. I thought about straightening my hair, which would be a three-hour process, but what about the humidity? What if it rained? Hours of hard work down the drain. Plus, I was too nervous to concentrate. I thought about going back to the pool, but I was too nervous to read, so I flicked on the TV and started to watch re-runs of *The Brady Bunch*.

That passed the time perfectly.

After several episodes, I fell asleep and woke up to the sound of my grandfather typing away on his laptop.

"What time is it?" I asked through a stretch and a yawn.

"6:38." he replied.

"6:38!" I exclaimed, completely panic-stricken. "Wha? How did that happen? I have to be ready in twenty-two minutes!"

"Ready for what, sweet-pea?" my oblivious grandfather asked.

"Shit!" I yelled as I my head spun around the room.

"Hey, watch it, young lady!" he said, his eyeglasses were drawn to his nose. "None of that kind of talk in my house!"

"Sorry…why didn't anyone wake me up?" I asked, frantically searching through the pile of clothes that I'd chosen.

"Well I didn't know that you had plans, first of all, and second of all, you looked so cute, lying there, just like you did when you were a baby… Oh, you had the cutest pudgy cheeks, and your curly hair would lie softly on your forehead." he said smiling.

"Grandpa!" I yelled.

"What?" he yelled back.

"I have a date in twenty-one minutes!"

"Well, what are you wasting your time talking to me for? You better get a move on!"

I scooped up my clothes and ran into the bathroom. I was moving so quickly that I shampooed my body and put soap in my hair. After I rinsed out the suds, I put a huge blob of conditioner to counteract my stupid mistake.

As I was toweling off, I noticed a bottle of body cream from Calvin Klein on the counter. I opened the bottle and it exploded all over the counter and onto the tiles on the floor. So much for smelling like a Calvin Klein model. I picked up my watch. It read 6:47.

"Shit!" I yelled.

"Hey!" my grandfather yelled from the other room.

"Sorry!" I called, as I grabbed the hand towels from the sink. I started to clean up the goop, but it just got smeared around.

In a panic mode, I got dressed.

I ran into my room with sopping wet hair while wearing damp clothes because I hadn't done a good job toweling off. I glanced in the mirror and saw that my cheeks were as red as two pomegranates, and my hair was as frizzy as a Brillo pad.

"Shit!" I said again.

"Ms. Elizabeth Stein! Do I need to wash out your mouth with soap?!" my grandfather yelled.

"Sorry!" I called again.

I looked at my watch. It was 6:55. I gelled my hair, took a fresh towel to pat my cheeks with, and then put on some cold cream. I swiped on some mascara and some lip gloss. I looked in the mirror and decided that I'd made a vast improvement. I didn't look half bad.

Then the doorbell rang.

My mother answered the door. I could hear Jimmy talking with her as I went back to the bathroom to clean up the mess I had made.

Then I walked to the front hallway and kissed my mother goodbye.

As we walked to the car, where Jimmy's brother Joshua stood holding the back door open for us, I was beaming.

"Someone is happy," Jimmy said.

"I think I just broke the world record for getting ready," I said proudly.

When we got to the theatre, I was too nervous and too exhausted to eat anything, so we took our seats right away.

"I want M&M's," Jimmy said.

I smiled. Out of all the candy that was available at the concession stand, he chose M&M's: What were the chances? What were the chances that I was at a movie with Jimmy? The list could go on.

He went to get them and when he returned, he offered some to me, but I refused. I couldn't deal with M&M's and Jimmy at the same time.

He shrugged and rested the bag of M&M's on my leg.

I translated that gesture to a holding-hands thing even though we weren't officially holding hands. I was relieved that we weren't, actually, because my hands were as clammy as a dog's nose.

After the movie, Jimmy walked me to the front door of the apartment. As our lips parted, he squeezed my shoulder and said goodnight. I didn't say anything because my mouth didn't work.

I opened the door, walked inside, and took a deep breath. Everyone was watching TV, and they all turned to me, smiling.

I smiled back.

My parents looked worried. But Lee said, "Relax guys; for the last time, she did not have sex!"

"Have sex?" my grandmother screamed.

"Who's having sex?" my grandfather yelled.

"Nobody, Grandpa. It was just some ugly rumour that a bunch of my friends made up."

"Some friends," my grandfather said.

Chapter 22

The next morning, I opened my eyes to see Lee standing over my bed, but thankfully not so early this time.

"It's great to see you smile again," He said.

"Yeah, I've been doing that a lot lately," I said. I stretched, smiled, and turned to look out the window.

"What time is it?" I asked, getting out of bed.

"A little after nine," Lee said.

"Mmm."

"Have fun last night?" Lee asked.

"Yeah."

"Good."

I turned around and looked at Lee. He was wearing his running outfit. He was such a caring older brother, always on top of things. Too annoyingly perfect. He was giving me one of those I-am-concerned-about-you looks.

"Thanks for last night," I said.

"Don't mention it," he said.

I walked out of the bedroom.

"Hey, where are you going?" Lee asked.

"To get some OJ before my run," I said.

"I've created a monster!"

"Yes, you have!"

* * *

After my run and a bowl of oatmeal with blueberries, I met Jimmy by the pool, where we let our feet dangle in the water.

"Ever think about your friends?" He asked.

"What friends?" I said.

"Don't want to go there?"

"Not really."

"Why?"

I shrugged.

He nodded.

"Well, if you ever want to."

I looked up at him and smiled.

After lunch, I went to the flea market with my mother and grandmother, and it was a madhouse. There must have been a million people there. Everywhere you turned, there was someone bargaining prices down and hordes of people carrying parcels bigger than their bodies.

I bought some gym socks, jogging T-shirts, and shorts, because if I was going to become a runner, I was certainly going to dress the part. When we got home, I put them on, and somehow I felt different. I looked like a runner. I also noticed that I had some new muscles in my calves, and I thought about going to my weigh-in next week.

The following night, Jimmy and I went for a walk after dinner. When I got home at 10:30 pm, my mother looked at me. "Nice time?" she asked.

"Yep."

"I just wanted to let you know that I believe that you didn't have sex with Jimmy."

"I know."

"And I hope he's not asking you to do something that you are not comfortable with."

"Mom."

"We don't have to talk about sex itself. Even if it's just talking, holding hands and kissing"

"I get the picture. Look, I'm fine, and I'll let you know if I need anything. Okay?"

"Okay."

Jimmy and I spent the majority of our time together sitting on the beach, staring into the ocean. We didn't say much. We held hands, and he kissed me goodnight at my front door. I could have told my mother this, but I didn't want to.

* * *

December 25th, Christmas day. Everything was closed, because the majority of the world was sipping eggnog and ripping wrapping paper off of their presents. For the rest of us—Jews and Muslims, mostly— well, we went to the movies or just hung around. Very few businesses were open, but Fatty Club was, so I decided to hop on their scale and catch a flick afterwards.

"Okay, get on," the weight attendant said.

I stepped on the cold, metal frame.

"Down three," She whispered.

"Woo hoo!" I hooted.

"Okay, calm down, there tiger," She said.

"Sorry, just very excited. Say, you must be Jewish or Muslim to be working today, right?" I said with an expression that was way too happy.

"Yes, I am Jewish," she said just above a monotone.

"Me too! Coooool," I said again, way to happy.

She smiled and shook her head like I belonged in the looney bin, but I didn't care. I was half way to my goal weight.

Later that afternoon we all went to a movie. Mom snuck in sandwiches for lunch in her purse. Then we drove to the airport to pick up Linda. Lee was happy to see her and so was I, because her arrival meant he could stop bugging me about running with him—I preferred running alone. And I did just that, the minute we got home.

"Where are you going?" Linda asked.

"Running," I said.

"Really?" she asked, reacting as if I'd just told her I'd decided to join a cult.

"Really."

"By yourself."

"Uh-huh," I said, lacing up my shoes.

"Without Lee?"

"Oh, yeah," I said, noticeably relieved, and ran out the front door.

When I got home, I peeled off my clothes and hopped into the shower. As I was toweling off, there was a banging at the door.

"Whaaaat?" I yelled annoyed.

"Movie in half an hour," Lee yelled through the door.

"But we already went to one today!" I yelled back.

"Jimmy's coming. He called while you were in the shower, and Linda invited him. Merry Christmas!"

My grin was so wide it burned my cheeks. I couldn't help it. I was so excited to see him again.

After I tried to tame my nest of hair into some orderly arrangement, I got dressed. Soon, the three of us were in the elevator, heading to meet Jimmy in our lobby.

"Lizzie and Jimmy, sitting in a tree, K-I-S-S-I-N-G!" Lee joked.

"Come on Lee, leave her alone," Linda said.

"Does he kiss good, Lizzie?" Lee whispered.

"Does he kiss well," I corrected. "Didn't you take English 101 at school you math freak?"

"Whatever. Does he make your knees melt?"

"Knock it off!" I yelled.

"Does he put his hand on your ass?" Lee continued. "Because if he does, I'll kill him."

"Please stop. Just stop."

The elevator stopped and the doors opened. Jimmy was standing in the lobby, smiling.

"What were you guys yelling about? I heard you all the way from your floor."

"Politics," I said, frowning.

"It's a double date!" Lee announced with is arms in the air. "Whoo hooooo!" he said as he swung his hips.

Jimmy and I ignored him and walked to the car.

"I've got to see you get it on with lover-lips in the back seat," Lee said.

"I am going to have to kill you, very soon," I threatened.

"Lee, stop it," Linda pleaded. "It's enough."

Jimmy giggled to himself.

"But it's so much fun to watch Lizzie turn purple."

"You know, I totally lost my tan today from sitting in a movie theatre," I butted in, trying to change the subject.

"No you didn't." Jimmy said, and he stroked my cheek. There I was, turning purple, just like Lee wanted to see me do.

The movie theatre was pretty busy. We managed to get four seats in a row, but they were off to the side. During the previews, a commercial came on and my eyes nearly popped out of my head. The girl who was selling the sugar-free gum looked exactly like Amanda.

"Hey, she looks like Amanda!" Jimmy whispered in my ear.

Then of course, all sorts of thoughts started repeating in my head, and I missed a great movie. The audience was roaring with laughter, but all I could do was sit there thinking about Amanda, Lisa, Gail, the ugly rumour, garbage in my locker, and the intercom.

After the movie, we went for frozen yogurt.

Linda said, "So, Lizzie, how's your Fatty Club going?"

I could have killed her. Sometimes she said things without thinking, and it drove me totally bonkers. And why did frozen yogurt always make people think of dieting? Why couldn't a person just sit and enjoy the calcium?

"It's called Frieda's," I corrected her.

"You go there? Frieda's Fatty Club?" Jimmy interjected. "Uh, I mean - Frieda's Happy Losers. My mom went there, and she lost a lot of weight!"

I nodded, wondering if I should invest in a purple blouse to match my face.

"I can't believe you do that sort of thing! Isn't it only for, like, older... fat people?" He asked.

"Oh, no. Anyone can join," I quietly said, still very purple.

"But you're not fat," Jimmy said, looking confused.

"My doctor thought it was a good idea," I quietly said, hoping to end the conversation. As soon as possible.

Jimmy furrowed his brows.

Jimmy held my hand in the car. Lee and Linda went upstairs to the apartment, and Jimmy and I sat outside for a while. Then he walked me up to the apartment and I invited him inside for a drink. Everyone was asleep, and Lee and Linda were nowhere to be found.

We walked to the pantry to get the extra bottle of cranberry juice. I started to chat. "Linda sleeps with me in the guest room and man does she snore." I began. "And she..." But I couldn't talk anymore, because Jimmy reached for my neck and brought my face to meet his. He gently pressed his lips to mine and I wrapped my arms around his neck and ran my fingers through his hair. I felt that I was floating above sea level until out of nowhere I started to think about someone deciding that they wanted a drink, a cookie, or some cereal? I broke away from him and he gave me a confused look.

Suddenly a door shut and I jumped out of the pantry. I ran to the cupboard to get a glass and immediately started to pour the cranberry juice. I held onto the glass and smiled.

"Hey guys!" Lee said. He had rumpled hair.

"Did a raccoon go through your hair?" I joked, knowing very well that Linda was the culprit. I wanted to get him back for putting me through the embarrassing double date extravaganza earlier.

"Touché, Lizzie." Lee poured himself a glass of juice. He looked at Jimmy and me as he gulped. We smiled back at him. He finally finished and put the empty glass down on the counter.

"You guys okay?" he asked.

"Oh, yeah," I said.

"Great," Jimmy said.

"Thanks for driving us to the movie," Jimmy said.

"No problem. Glad you guys had fun." Lee walked back to his bedroom.

Jimmy and I shrugged and smiled, and then I walked him to the door to say goodbye.

Chapter 23

The next day all I did was think about kissing Jimmy in the pantry. I was practically banging into walls.

"Are you alright?" my grandmother asked me.

"Oh, yeah. Just fine."

"Did you have a nice time last night, with that young man? Jimmy, right?"

"Yes, Grandma," I said with an impatient tone.

"Don't 'Yes, Grandma' me, young lady. I wasn't born yesterday," she said. "I can always smell something cooking in the kitchen."

I didn't know what to say.

But I did know what to do: go shopping with Linda. After all, it was Boxing Day.

"Who wants to go shopping today?" I yelled from the kitchen, hoping Linda would hear me. In ten seconds, I heard her feet run down the hallway and the jingle of car keys in her hand.

"Good," my grandmother said. "Go. Have fun."

Linda appeared in the kitchen as if she was a five-year-old being told that she was going to the park.

"Let's go!" she said, smiling.

As we walked through the mall, I had to hold onto Linda's arm because it was so crowded. She dragged me into a shoe store and put a pair of loafers in my hand.

"Okay, Lizzie, let's talk about your shoe situation."

"But I love my Keds!" I whined.

"Yes," she said, "but there are other shoes in this world, you know."

"But these aren't as comfy," I said, holding the loafers.

"These are dressier shoes. You'll get used to them."

I made a face.

"Look, I'm not asking you to wear four-inch heels, Lizzie. Just try them on," she said.

"Okay," I said. "At least they're on sale."

As I strolled through the mall, I continued to hold her arm.

"You look good," she said.

"Well, I lost about eight pounds."

"No, it's not that. I mean it's more than that. You're glowing on the inside."

"Wha?"

"Love," Linda said knowingly.

"No way," I said.

"Trust me, I know. Now, let's get some jeans for Lightbulb Lizzie."

Inside The Limited, I went to the jeans section and took out a pair. A sales clerk came by.

"Whoa, there," she warned. "Those are way too big for you. Try the eight."

"Eight?"

"Eight."

"Eight?"

"Eight!"

"Okay," I said totally confused and went to the dressing room. Linda waited patiently outside.

"Wow. Two whole sizes down." I said as I came out of the dressing room.

"Cool!" said Linda.

"They look good," I said.

"Yep."

"Fifty percent off, too!" I squealed.

"Okay! Let's pay and get out of this madhouse."

On our way out, we stopped at the cosmetic counter and Linda got a bottle of her favourite perfume, which came with a gift.

"Here," she said, and handed me a fancy bag with a big red bow on top.

"What's this?" I asked.

"Gift with purchase! I want you to have it. I have enough cosmetic junk at home and, well, you've been through some pretty heavy stuff and worked hard these past couple of months."

"But it's your favourite cosmetic company!" I said, then opened the bag and looked inside. "There's even a travel-size version of your perfume."

"I know," she said with the smile she gives Lee when she sees him.

When I got home, I ran to my room to look at my new clothes and inspect all the other goodies in the gift bag Linda had given me. The lipstick was orange, the cream was for wrinkles that I didn't have, and I really didn't like the perfume that she wore. But I didn't care. I was beaming inside because Linda thought I deserved it.

* * *

A few days later it was New Year's Eve. Jimmy and I decided that we were going to order pizza and watch the ball drop in New York City on TV. Everyone was going out to a party at the clubhouse, except for Lee and Linda, who were going to a bar because they had fake IDs.

Before Jimmy came over, I decided to call Jenny Goldberg. She had two weeks off and was spending them at our country house. I told her about everything—the weather, the shopping, the pantry scene, and the final comment from my grandmother about cooking in the kitchen.

"No way, she didn't say that!" Jenny screamed through the phone so loudly that I had to pull the receiver away from my ear.

"Yes way!" I said.

"Hey, you'd better be careful next time," said Jenny. "If I were you, I'd take the lip-locking outside."

"You're right," I agreed.

Silence.

"Did you and Jimmy talk about, you know, the rumour, the humiliation on the school intercom? Your hospital visit?"

"No, no, no and no," I said bluntly.

"Are you going to?"

"Dunno."

"How would you even bring it up?" she asked.

"Good question."

We chatted for a little while longer. She told me about the Christmas concert she had performed in, explaining that after she had curtsied, she had tripped on her skirt and fallen off the stage into someone's lap.

"Ooh, that's bad," I said.

"You're telling me!"

We said our goodbyes, and I hopped in the shower.

Everyone went out at 7:00 pm, and I was left to finish getting dressed. I put on my new jeans and a T-shirt, smoothed my hair with gel, put on some lip gloss and I even put on a little mascara and some blush: heck, it was New Year's Eve. I was ready for Jimmy's arrival by 7:30, and my heart was doing flip-flops.

When Jimmy showed up, I was beaming inside. His hair was still wet from his shower (just like mine). He was wearing his Levis and a T- shirt, and he had the cutest little sunburn across his nose. Right away he came over and hugged me. It was weird: I was excited to be close to him, yet scared at the same time. He held my head in his hands and kissed me and said: "I'm starving!" I took his hand and tugged him into the kitchen to call for pizza.

While we were waiting, I made a tossed salad and some iced tea. We watched some American music station while we were waiting for our pizza. Madonna was on, and I insisted that we watch because my mom had done Baby-and-Me aerobics classes to her music when I was an infant. My mom told me that I'd always have a huge smile on my face whenever Madonna was played, and that has made me a fan ever since. In the middle of her classic 80s' tune "Holiday" I blurted out:

"Did you have anything to do with that rumour, back in October?"

Jimmy seemed taken aback. "Excuse me?"

I stared at him.

"Uh, no," he said.

"Really?" I asked.

"Really. But, you know, I really don't care."

"What do you mean you don't care?"

"Because it's not true, so why should I care? Why do you care?"

"Well, my whole reputation was taken to the cleaners, for one thing."

"But if you knew it wasn't true and you let everyone know that by your reactions, then it doesn't matter."

"Are you for real?"

"Think so."

"I guess guys are different that way."

"You can say that again."

I thought about it for the length of three commercials. I found it absolutely amazing that he could ignore the whole rumour and get on with his life while I let it eat at me like mosquitoes on a perfumed wrist.

"What about the intercom thing?" I probed.

"I had absolutely nothing to do with that one, but I can tell you one thing," Jimmy began. "That day did suck for me. All my friends were teasing me about it. But I decided to forget about it so it would go away. And it did. Over. Done. Finished."

"Once again, guys are so different."

I decided to save the topic of my hospital visit for another time. Didn't want to bombard him with too much information for one evening.

"Okay, so what do we do when we get back?" I asked.

"Go to school," he said.

"No!" I said shyly. "I mean…you know…"

He laughed. "You mean, am I your boyfriend?"

"Yeah."

"Of course. What do you think? Geez, you girls always need everything spelled out for you."

"It was just one question!"

Jimmy lifted his pizza to take a bite and it slipped out of his hands and fell on the floor. We ran to the kitchen to grab soda water and started scrubbing. It mostly came out. We had a good laugh and finished our dinner.

I think I ate too quickly because I ended up getting a stomach ache. For the rest of the evening, I lay down with my legs on his lap. While we watched the ball drop, he massaged my feet.

* * *

Before we left Florida, it was time for another weigh-in. I had lost another pound. Lee took it as a personal accomplishment. "It was all the running that made the difference," he boasted.

For our final night, I went out for a quick dinner with my parents and then I met Jimmy for our last movie together in Florida. We held hands during the entire movie, and my hands weren't sweaty at all. I was relaxed, and this time I actually paid attention to the movie.

Afterwards, we took a walk on the beach, and I felt like I was in the middle of a movie scene. I loved holding his hand and watching the wind blow through his hair. I tried not to stare at him too often, but I couldn't help it. When we got back, he rinsed my feet with the beach hose.

It was time to say goodbye to Florida, face my demons, and begin opening my heart to a complete stranger: Marna, the therapist my mom had set me up with. It all seemed incredibly overwhelming.

Jimmy was staying in Florida through the next weekend for his cousin's bar mitzvah ceremony, and I told him to take pictures for me. He had my heart wrapped around his little finger. This vacation had been exactly what I needed.

On the plane ride home there was so much turbulence, I didn't know what to do with myself. I read my *People* magazine eight times, and I listened to my iPod, but all I could think about was that I didn't have a will. All I had were teddy bears, some nice sweaters, and the pearls I was wearing around my neck. If I had a will, I would give my *Seventeen* magazine collection to Jenny and instruct her to burn my math books.

When I got home, safe and sound, I unpacked my clothes and went through my mail. I picked out my clothes for the next morning and made my lunch. I was all set. I only wished my books, clothes, and lunch could get up and walk to school without me, and that I could stay at home all safe and warm in my bed.

Chapter 24

The next morning, I was walking to my bus stop while listening to one of my favourite songs. While I was boogying to the beat of the music, I slipped on a sheet of ice and slid into a mushy puddle of snow. My pants were soaked, so I had to rush home and quickly change, which put me way off my morning schedule.

I ended up at school just a few seconds shy of the first-period bell. I really hoped this incident didn't foreshadow the theme for the rest of the school year.

As I was shoving my coat and boots into my locker, I noticed Lisa and Gail standing by theirs, just a few doors down.

"You look good, Lizzie," Lisa said.

"Thanks," I said. I couldn't tell if I was sweating because I was nervous or because of my mad dash to change from wet to dry clothes. I also wondered why Lisa had paid me a compliment. It was too nice to be true.

I took my seat in my homeroom classroom, and our teacher announced that she would be distributing our exams. I couldn't have cared less, because all I could think about was surviving the day. Was David going to pop out of nowhere and swing me around? Was Amanda going to announce something again on the intercom? Who cared about exams? The only one I really cared about was math, which was the academic devil of my high school education so far.

My English exam appeared on my desk. I shoved it in my binder and didn't even look at the grade. I was too nervous thinking about what was going to happen after this period, which was study hall. When the warning bell rang for first period to end, I decided to go right to my third period class, which was math, and have a chit-chat with Mr. Drane. Maybe even get my exam back early. I was hoping for a miracle on that one.

When I got to the classroom, Mr. Drane was busy looking over the exams and almost seemed to be in another world. I knocked.

"Hey! Nice tan," he smiled.

"Thanks," I said.

"How are you doing?"

"Great," I said, not sounding it.

"You look worried."

"Why, should I be worried?"

"I don't know. Why should you be worried?"

"I am not talking about my grades here, because I know we have some work to do this winter," I explained.

"That's right," he agreed.

My stomach turned into a prune. I knew a bad mark was coming, but I was hoping that I would slip by with a passing mark. Mr. Drane realized that I was starting to panic, so he quickly changed the subject.

"Okay, math aside, what else is going on?"

"I got to school this morning and Lisa gave me a compliment. She said that I looked good."

"That's great," he said. "Maybe she's coming around."

"I don't know; it just doesn't sit right."

"Well, didn't they do enough to you already?"

"I just feel that something is up," I admitted.

"Look," Mr. Drane began, comforting me. "They got in pretty deep trouble in November, so maybe they've had enough of you."

I guess," I sulked. "I, uh…I'm going to start seeing someone about all of this."

Mr. Drane noticed my eyes tearing up. He smiled. Introduction to therapy with the math teacher.

"You okay with that?" he asked.

"Do I have a choice?"

"Well—my guess is 'no?'"

"You got it."

"Why don't you—" he began.

The bell rang.

"Sorry, you gotta go. Eighth-graders will be pouring in here any minute," he said, and smiled apologetically. I took my books and weaved my way through the flood of bodies that came into the classroom like a tidal wave.

I stood alone in the hallway, not knowing where to go.

Mr. Drane opened his classroom door.

"Get in here."

"Thanks!" I said, confused and relieved, and I entered his classroom.

"Ladies and gentlemen, I present to you Lizzie Stein, Math Whiz of the Ninth Grade. She's here this morning for research."

The whole class turned around to look at me, and I smiled like I was Miss America. Was I happy to be there? Not really. But it was better than standing in the hallway, dreading study hall.

When the class was over, I went up to Mr. Drane and thanked him. And then he excused himself to refill his coffee mug.

I took my seat and waited for the class to fill up. In walked Amanda. She didn't look like herself. She was wearing a plain white T-shirt and blue jeans. No flashy necklaces, no earrings, no bright-coloured sweater that was two sizes too small. Her hair was in a low ponytail, and she had no makeup on—not even lip gloss. Her facial expression was as bland as white rice.

"Hi," she said as she took a seat behind me.

"Hi," I was feeling extremely confused. Why did she want to sit next to me, and why was she talking to me?

"Nervous?" she asked.

"I guess," I said.

Mr. Drane came back into the classroom, took a sip from his mug, and started to hand out exams. One by one he called people's names. My heart was doing leaps and somersaults in my body. I took a deep breath and decided to talk to Amanda again.

"Have a nice break?" I asked.

"It sucked, really," she replied, just above a whisper.

My exam appeared on my desk with a huge red "47%" marked on it. I could feel myself turning white. I looked at Mr. Drane, hoping for a don't-worry-it's-going-to-be-alright look. But there was no consolation.

"People, we don't have time to go over the exam because we have to finish this course ASAP," Mr. Drane announced. "So please see me after class if you have any questions regarding your exam."

Amanda laughed when she saw my grade. "Well, that mark sucks just like my vacation!"

I really wanted to take Amanda's finger and shove it into the classroom pencil sharpener.

Aside from my pathetic math situation and my stupid conversation with Amanda, no one bothered me about my supposedly active sex life. I guess the holiday break had erased it from their minds. I decided to forget the whole thing, just like Jimmy had, because it simply wasn't true. But I still couldn't get the intercom prank out of my head. That did happen. When the dismissal bell rang at 3:30 pm sharp, I ran down the hallway, whipping past David. As soon as he saw me, he ran after me. I kept running, bolted through the front doors, and ran to the bus stop, trying not to slip on the ice. I turned around—no David—and breathed a sigh of relief. Thankfully, I caught the bus before the crowds came. Why the rush? I had my very first appointment with Marna, and I didn't want to be late.

When I got off the bus, I ran into the mall and dashed towards the office elevators, praying that I wouldn't be seen by anyone I knew. I walked into Marna's office and plopped myself down on her waiting room couch. She had some great *Archie* comic books in her waiting room, dating back to the 1970s. I wondered if they were hers.

The door finally opened, and a woman who seemed way older than me, but much younger than my mom, called my name. She was wearing a bright-orange, wool dress and black tights. Her hair was as black as her tights and hung straight and smooth right down to her lower back. I stared at it with envy. I would have loved to trade in my frizzy massive curls for her super-shiny straight hair.

"Welcome," she said in a soft voice.

"Thanks," I said.

I got up and walked into her office. She didn't have the type of couch that you saw on TV, the kind that was leather and looked like a bed with an armrest on the side. It was a regular couch that you would see in anyone's living room. She pulled the chair that sat by her desk towards the couch where I sat, and slipped off her shoes. She looked straight into my eyes and smiled.

"Get here okay?" she asked.

"Oh yeah, I took the 161," I said in a shaky voice. "It lets me right off in front. Convenient."

"You can't drive yet, right?" Marna asked.

"No, not until next year. I highly doubt that I would even get a car. I would probably have to borrow one from one of my parents, maybe share one with Lee, my brother. We'll see."

I was rambling. I went on. "You know, I can't imagine sharing a car with Lee. He always has hockey practice, fraternity parties... I mean, when would I get the car? Probably never. Total car hog, my brother."

I looked around her office and noticed some stuffed animals sitting on her desk.

"Okay, that's weird," I said, nodding at them.

"Oh, those. They stand for people who have influenced my life. The top two are well-known psychologists, Sigmund Freud and Abraham Maslow. And the one sitting in front of them is named Dr. Brown—he was my favourite professor in graduate school."

I nodded and smiled.

"Lizzie, do you know why you are here?" Marna asked.

It came out of nowhere. I started to sniffle, and then the tears came rolling down my cheeks, and they wouldn't stop. Marna whipped a box of Kleenex in front of my nose and placed it on my lap for the entire hour. I just had a good, old-fashioned, nose-dripping, hysterical cry. I calmed down after my hour was up. I looked at her.

"Am I going to do this every time?" I asked. "I didn't get a chance to say anything!"

She reached into her drawer and pulled out a bottle of eye-makeup remover, a cotton ball, and a small mirror. "Here, you need this. You look like a raccoon."

I took it and started to clean up my face.

"This happens a lot, in the beginning," she said. "Once we've met a few more times, we'll talk more. About the real 'stuff.'"

"Okay," I said, shaking.

"When you get home, you are going to be exhausted," Marna warned.

I looked at her, confused.

"You just let out a huge amount of tension, and your body has to recuperate. You've been through a lot, you know."

I nodded and took a deep breath.

"Okay, go home, get some rest. You may not be able to do your homework, so when you see me next week, try and get as much work done before you see me so you can go home and just chill."

"Okay," I said. I felt completely overwhelmed.

"See you soon, raccoon!" Marna joked.

"Uh, yeah," I still felt confused.

I walked out of her office like a zombie. I decided to walk home in the blistering wind. I couldn't face anyone, and I just wanted to walk and think. To think what, I had no idea.

Chapter 25

The whole next week of school, during lunch, I noticed that Amanda was keeping to herself. She sat by her locker and read. I didn't see her eat, talk to anyone, or move except to turn a page. Just before the bell rang, she went to the bathroom and then got her books out of her locker for the next class. How did I know her every move without her knowing? I would occasionally check up on her while I ate my lunch on my own lunch throne, the beloved toilet flusher.

Marna wanted to see me weekly, so before I had a chance to turn around, I was on the bus again, skipping my stop to go to her office. The next session we just sat and talked about things like my family, school, and my fear of numbers. Then, after forty-five minutes, I started to talk about LAG.

"What's a LAG?" Marna asked.

"Oh, an acronym for Lisa, Amanda, and Gail. There's a David there too, but he doesn't fit into the acronym, so I just mention David separately."

She smiled and nodded.

Pause. I smiled.

"So, what about them?" she asked.

"What do you want to know?"

"Up to you."

I thought about it.

"Well, they used to be my best friends. And, well, now they're not."

"Do you know why that is?" she asked.

I shook my head and raised my shoulders.

"Any idea?" she urged.

"Well, things just got weird when I got home from camp."

"What do you mean by 'weird?'"

"Well, Lisa, Amanda, and Gail would smoke and stuff."

"Let's first start with the smoking. Before we get to the 'stuff,'" Marna suggested.

"Okay," I said, feeling like we were going somewhere.

"Do you think smoking is bad?"

"Well, health-wise, yes, but socially, I guess not."

"So, why is their smoking a problem?"

"Well, I just didn't want to do it."

"And they made you?"

'No...they made me feel uncomfortable if I didn't," I explained. "You see, I can't inhale right because I start to choke. It's a whole big mess."

"So how did they make you feel?" she asked.

"Left out," I said softly.

She nodded.

"Okay, what about the 'stuff?'" Marna continued.

"Well, they were being mean. Making fun of my weight, telling lies, spreading rumours." I looked down at the carpet.

"That's horrible."

"Yeah," I agreed. "And... I started to like this really cute guy, and then just because Amanda liked him too, they all started to gang up on me!"

"Horrible again!"

"I know! We were at this party and I was completely exposed from "

I stopped short. I realized where my story was going and I wasn't ready to tell Marna about the bathroom scene yet.

"Exposed from what?" Marna asked.

"Just exposed," I said. She nodded.

"I was left alone." I said.

"Where were your friends?"

I didn't answer. I looked away.

"Does this 'exposed' thing mean that you had sex?" Marna asked gently.

"No! I did not have sex! Why does everybody think that?" I yelled. "We were just kissing in the bathroom!"

"Okay, okay. I just had to ask."

I sighed heavily.

Marna looked at her watch.

"We'll continue this next week," she said.

"But I was just getting started!"

"I know, don't worry. We'll get it all covered."

When I got home I was famished. Mom made turkey burgers, and I devoured mine like an animal.

When I went to weigh-in that week, I had stayed the same, which I was totally fine about. As long as I was heading in the right direction, I was in no rush. Plus, I didn't want to draw any more attention to myself.

* * *

The following week, Jimmy returned from Florida. I met him in the hallway, just outside the front doors of the school, before first period.

"Hey!" he said with his arms opened.

"Hi!" I said as I embraced him.

It was a bit awkward, on my part, but still warm at the same time. It was different. We were at school and not on the beach.

"Welcome home," I said.

"Thanks."

"How was the bar mitzvah ceremony?"

"Sokay."

We started to walk towards his locker.

"You should have been my date."

"Rain check. Had to get back. Can't miss a moment of math."

"Ugh, that reminds me. I missed a whole week of school," he said. The bell rang and off we went to class.

On my way home, I saw David out of the corner of my eye, but I ran full speed ahead to the front door of the school. Then I felt like running even more, so I kept running, past the bus stop and onto the sidewalk. People kept calling out, "What's the rush?" and "Where's your train?"

I ignored them and kept on going, breaking through the January wind, stopping at traffic lights, going through two underpasses, and then finally heading towards the familiar streets where I felt safe. When I reached my house, I felt great, but my back did not. My school bag had been bumping up and down on my back while I ran, so when I took off my sweatshirt to take a shower my whole back was sweaty and red.

Later on that afternoon, the phone rang in the middle of my strange but welcome desire to finish a math problem.

"Why didn't you wait for me after school today?" Jimmy asked fearlessly.

"You didn't ask me to," I quivered, knowing that I didn't need to be asked.

"Oh, okay," he said softly.

"Can you meet me tomorrow?" I asked.

"Sure, and want to come over to my house for dessert on Friday night?" he asked.

"Love to," I said beaming.

Chapter 26

"Your buttons are all screwed up," Lee informed me at breakfast the next morning.

"Wha?" I looked down from my bowl of cereal and shrugged. I got up from the table and fixed my shirt in front of the hallway mirror.

"Something on your mind?" Lee shouted from the table.

"Leave her alone," my dad warned.

I returned to the kitchen table, gulped down my orange juice, and took off for school.

Not something, I thought to myself; someone.

I had already seen Jimmy at school. I'd had a weird, icky feeling in my stomach—from the change of being on the beach with him to being at school with him—yet I was excited to go to his house on Friday night. My feelings were all over the place; it was much easier being alone in my bathroom stall or in Mr. Drane's classroom during lunch.

As the morning progressed at school, instead of growling for lunch as usual, my stomach was turning in circles. When the bell finally rang, my heart started to pound.

"Hey!" Jimmy's voice said behind me as I was putting my books away in my locker.

"Hi," I said.

"I'll trade you half my tuna on kimmel bread for whatever you've got."

"I've got tuna on black."

"Cool. I love bread," he said.

"Me too," I said, smiling, feeling not so nervous anymore.

"Let's eat in the caf," he said as I closed my locker. "Then I've got to mosey to the physics lab."

"Ooh, can I come?" I asked sarcastically.

In the middle of the enormous lunchroom, filled with over a thousand students, we found a spot for two, right in the middle. I bit into his sandwich.

"What's in here?" I asked.

"My mom's secret ingredient," he said.

"Which is?"

"If I tell you, I'd have to kill you."

I smiled as he bit into my half. He gestured towards the sandwich, wondering what was in mine.

"I'm not telling. And I will ask your mother myself this Friday," I said smugly.

I looked around the cafeteria nervously. "You okay?" he asked.

I nodded and put my sandwich down.

"I just want to be back in Florida, with no outsiders. Just you and me." I couldn't believe I'd just said that.

"I know. It's easier that way," he said. "I know I said in Florida that it doesn't matter because what they were spreading around wasn't true, but I will admit that it bothers me that some people still stare."

"Wow. That's the first time you're admitting this," I said.

"I know."

"In Florida," I went on, "there's no Lisa, Amanda, Gail, or David."

"And no snow," Jimmy interrupted.

"Oh, I don't mind the snow."

"The skier that you are," he said. I smiled.

"Let's just take it slow, okay? We don't have to eat lunch together every day," he said. "Just let me know when you're free and I'll have my secret tuna sandwich all ready for you."

"Great," I said with relief.

"You know," Jimmy said then, "you don't have to go to Drane for math. I could help you."

"Yeah," I agreed, then added wryly, "... but we wouldn't get anything done."

* * *

Even if you're a complete loner, like I was at the time, there is nothing like being fifteen with your parents out of town for the weekend. Off they went with the Goldbergs to the country with their guests and their fancy stinky cheeses and their many bottles of wine.

Lee and I went to Grandma's house for dinner on Friday night. I stared at my plate, which was filled with all of my favourite things: roasted turkey, mashed potatoes, and sautéed spinach.

"Leah-leh, what's the matter?" Grandma asked, calling me by my

Hebrew name, which she did from time to time. "Still watching your weight?"

"Eh," I replied.

Lee butted in, "She has a hot date for dessert."

I kicked Lee in the leg under the table and Grandma smiled with approval. "Is he a nice young man?"

"Very," I said.

"Well, you never know…" she said, trailing off.

"Meaning…?"

"Well, I met your Grandpa when I was twenty, and you're not far off from there," she said, winking.

"Uh, try five years!" I exclaimed, horrified.

"A lot could happen in five years!"

I thought about it and decided that having a plain ol' boyfriend sounded fine to me. I was not in the market for a husband. But Grandma, of course, got the last word.

"Well," she said, "you just never know."

Seven-thirty crept up pretty fast, and Lee said, "We'd better hit the road." We helped Grandma with the dishes, and went on our way.

In the car, I reached into my purse for my breath spray and lip gloss. Then I smoothed down my blow-dried hair—which had taken two freakin' hours to do—with my anti-frizz serum. I missed Lisa's expertise.

"Quit messing with your hair!" Lee yelled.

"Oh, blame it on Dad. He's the one who gave me his nest," I said.

We were in front of Jimmy's house by 8:00. His father opened the door, and inside sat about forty people! My heart sank to my feet as Dr.

Singer took my coat and I slipped off my boots. Jimmy got up from the table and greeted me with a kiss on the cheek.

"Nice hair!" he said.

"I've got the burning arms to prove it," I said.

Jimmy looked confused.

"Straight-haired creatures like you don't get it," I said.

As I took my place at the table, his whole family was smiling as if I was the queen or something. I turned eighty-seven shades of red. Jimmy had a chair waiting for me next to him, which made me feel more comfortable.

Mrs. Singer asked me how I liked school this year. I politely said it was okay, even though I could have talked her ear off about my gut-wrenching last five months. I wondered if she would have freaked out if I told her that I was seeing a shrink and that I preferred eating my lunch on the flusher of a toilet seat. I didn't tell her that. But I did have one question for her.

"Mrs. Singer, what do you put in your tuna salad?"

"Relish," she said plainly.

"Sneaky monster," Jimmy said.

"My mom uses dill and lemon juice," I announced. "Now we're even."

As I sipped my tea and had some pie, all sorts of questions started to pop up. "Do you go to Camp Winga? Because you look so familiar." "Does your mother shop at Parkview? I think I always see her on Friday mornings." The best one: "Hey, I see you every week at… oh, never mind." The relative who'd asked the question sank in her chair and an I'm-sorry-I embarrassed-you expression appeared on her face. She was referring to Frieda's Happy Losers.

After some more tuna salad recipe swapping, I took my tea cup and followed Jimmy and his cousin Calvin into the living room.

"Going out later?" Jimmy asked Calvin.

"Yup," Calvin said. "Picking up Hailey."

"Haven't heard about that one."

"She's my new flavour of the week," Calvin said proudly.

"Or day," Jimmy joked.

Calvin smirked as he raised his cup of tea to take a sip.

"Where are you going?" Jimmy asked.

"Dunno. Probably her house. In her basement. Alone."

"Have fun."

"Plan to," Calvin said as he took another sip of tea and turned his head to me at the same time. I swallowed hard, not knowing what was coming next from this playboy.

"And what about you, Mrs. Jimmy?" he asked, smiling.

"It's Lizzie," I said.

"Whatever. I call all of Jimmy's girls Mrs. Jimmy. Can't keep up."

I made a confused look.

"You know he's joking," Jimmy said. Calvin laughed. I was pissed off and I wanted to shut him up by whacking his face with my tea saucer.

"What about me?" I asked in a strong voice over his snarky, piggish laughter.

"What do you plan to do with my cousin this evening?" Calvin asked.

"Walk out of this living room," I said, getting up from my chair.

Jimmy smiled as we both walked out of the living room and left Calvin by himself.

A yawn sneaked out of my mouth.

"Tired?" Jimmy asked. I nodded. "Okay," he said. "Time to walk you home."

"You want to walk me home?" I yelled. "It's the middle of January!"

"You run home from school all the time," Jimmy pointed out.

"Yeah, but it's nighttime!" I argued, but I realized I was not going to win.

"Look, I'll lend you a pair of my wool socks, a sweater, a hat—the works," he said, and ran upstairs to get the extra layers while I said good-bye to his family.

By the time we were both in our winter layers, we looked like two abominable snowmen.

Thankfully, there was no wind outside. The snow glistened under the streetlamps and made a crunchy sound as we walked on the paved sidewalk. We held hands through our gloves. I decided right then and there that I wanted to tell Jimmy about Marna. I was ready, and my heart was pounding.

"I'm going somewhere once a week."

"Aren't you done with Frieda's?"

"No, not there. To a different place."

"You want to lose more weight?"

"No! It's not a weight thing!"

"Okay."

"It's a therapist."

"Oh."

Silence.

"There's my lack of friends, rumours, an uninvited intercom announcement, and the math thing. And, well, back in November, I kind of had a..."

"Nervous breakdown?"

"How'd you know?"

"I kind of figured."

"Oh." I looked down towards the snow, which I wanted to dig a hole in and hide.

"It's okay. Who cares? I mean, I care—but it's no big deal."

"It isn't?"

"Naw. What do you guys talk about?"

"Stuff."

"What kind of stuff?"

"Just stuff."

"Oh," Jimmy said gently. "Well, if you ever want to talk about 'stuff,' let me know."

"Cool." I smiled.

"I saw one once."

"You have? I asked with my eyes popped out of my head.

"My dog died when I was ten. My parents couldn't get me to leave his dog house in my back yard."

"You stayed there all day?"

"And all night."

I smiled at him.

"We all have our moments."

"I guess we do."

"I never told that to anyone before," he said.

I squeezed his hand. It was so reassuring that I was not the only one who was spending time on a shrink's couch. But really all I cared about was that he understood where I was coming from and that he still wanted to continue walking with me and not run away.

When we finally reached my house, he unzipped my coat and slipped his arms inside my jacket to hold me. I leaned in and kissed him, and he welcomed me with the strongest connection that was more powerful than I have ever felt before.

I felt my eyes fill up with tears, but thankfully they didn't trickle down my cheeks because I wasn't ready for him to see me cry. I went to bed that night holding his socks and sweater to my chest.

Chapter 27

As I got out of bed on Monday morning, all I could say was "SNOW!" Even though it was still dark, our house lights shone on the back yard, and everything I could see was white. It all looked beautiful, but I knew I had a treacherous journey to school that morning.

"I'll get my ski pants. I'm not getting my jeans soaked," I declared out loud to myself.

I went to school dressed like I was going to hit the slopes. David, of course, wasted no time informing me and everyone else around me of that.

"Hey!" he yelled. "Forget your skis?"

"Ha, ha," I laughed sarcastically.

As I took off my ski pants, he stood there, staring at me.

"Yes?" I asked, annoyed.

"Not bad, Lizzie."

"Wha?" I said, shocked and completely embarrassed.

"Mmm…" David said.

My eyes darted around. I really wanted to get out from under his gaze, but Amanda appeared behind David and he swung his head around to greet her, so I decided to stay. I had to admit, I was intrigued to hear her speak, since she hadn't been doing much of that lately.

"Hi," she said.

"Hey," David said.

I smiled at Amanda.

"Aren't you going to say hello to me?" she asked.

"Hi," I said softly. I got my books for my first class, closed my locker, and walked away, not smiling. I was on my way to the bathroom to check out the state of my eyeliner and hair, knowing that the weather had done a number on them on my way to school. As I was cleaning up my smudges and frizzes, Gail and Lisa walked into the reflection of my mirror. I stood up straight.

"Hi," Gail said.

I nodded.

"Uh, take it easy on Amanda, okay?" Lisa said.

"What do you mean, take it easy?" I asked, annoyed.

"She's just going through some…things, alright?"

"What kind of things?" I asked.

Lisa shrugged.

"But how do you expect me to be nice to her when…"

The bell rang, and the two of them ran out of the bathroom. I ran after them.

"Guys, wait!" I yelled.

They stopped in their tracks but were impatient.

"Why?" I asked. "Why should I be nice to her? Do you guys have short-term memory loss? Do I have to remind you?"

"Fine," Gail said. "Do what you want. We were just asking. It's the nice thing to do when your friend is in a crisis."

"Crisis? What the…"

I was unsuccessful at finishing my sentence because they both walked away, Gail leaning her head towards Lisa as she spoke in her ear. I stood there, in the middle of the hallway, motionless as the rest of the students bustled about, getting ready for class.

Jimmy called out from behind me. "Lizzie!" This made me smile.

"Good morning," I said.

"Hi," he said. He looked into my eyes and saw that I was not all right.

"What's brewing in your brain?" he asked.

"Oh, nothing," I lied.

"Want to talk about nothing over half of your favourite tuna sandwich?" he asked.

As I left him and went to my morning class, my head was so loaded that I couldn't concentrate on anything. It was a miracle I wasn't called on—but, just after the lunch bell rang and I was walking out the door, Mr. Drane came up to me.

"Where were you this period?" he asked. "Mars?"

"Yeah," I answered, "and I went to visit Pluto on the way."

Mr. Drane made a mean, scary look that slowly turned empathetic.

"What's going on?" he asked.

"Just got some stuff on my mind. Can't come to your clinic today. Tomorrow for sure."

"Fine."

"Thanks."

"I'll tutor her," Jimmy said as he approached the classroom to pick me up.

"Very funny," Mr. Drane said.

"No, I can do it," Jimmy protested.

"Can we just eat?" I said. "I'm so hungry."

"Yes, feed her," Mr. Drane said. "She needs the protein to concentrate in her classes. Unlike this morning in mine."

"Okay. Okay," I said on my way out of the classroom. "I will pay attention next time!"

Jimmy held out his hand for me to hold as we walked to the cafeteria, and I was more than happy to hold it. Once we sat down, I didn't say much. I just ate. Looked around and ate. Jimmy watched me. I finally spoke.

"Okay, Lisa and Gail told me to be nice to Amanda? Can you believe that?"

"That's weird!"

"I know!"

"Something is up."

"And I'm gonna find out," I vowed. Out of the corner of my eye I saw Lisa and Gail sitting at a nearby table. Lisa was eating a cup of noodles while Gail was pouring dressing on her salad. I wanted to talk to them again. Jimmy read my mind.

"Go. Now. And let me know what they said."

I nodded.

I nervously approached their table and sat down. I didn't receive the warmest reception as I sat, but they didn't ask me to leave either.

"Okay, what's going on?" I asked in a shaky voice.

No response.

"She needs her space right now," Lisa said.

"Amanda? Needs space?"

I made a confused face, knowing very well that Amanda thrived with people. Whenever she failed an exam, got dumped by a guy, or got caught cheating on a test, she used to grab me in the hallway or call me on the telephone, or show up at my door with her tales of misery. And I would patiently listen.

"Look, we're not at liberty to say anything right now," Lisa said and rolled her eyes.

"Oh come on," I said. "Don't give me that crap."

"Ask her yourself," said Gail with a mouthful of lettuce.

I got up and walked to the cafeteria doors, hoping to find Amanda where I'd seen her last week: by her locker, reading a book or something.

As I opened the heavy steel doors, there she was, looking right at me.

"My parents are getting a divorce," she said, point-blank.

Chapter 28

As Amanda stood outside of the cafeteria in the hallway, motionless, David's deep and raspy voice came closer.

"Heeeere's Lizzie!" he bellowed through the hallway. I didn't flinch; I was in total shock. I couldn't understand why Amanda was telling me, of all people, this terrible news. David started humming like he was the master of ceremonies on a late-night TV talk show.

"Lizzie?" Amanda asked.

"Da da da da da…" David sung.

"Mmm?" I asked, in a daze.

"Da da da da da da da…" David went on.

"Aren't you going to say anything?" Amanda asked.

"Say what?" David asked as the one-man orchestra approached us.

"Nothing," I said.

"What do you mean, 'nothing?'" David asked as he grabbed both of us and put his arms around our shoulders. "Hey. This is just like old times, eh, girls?" he said, smiling, showing all his teeth.

"Yep," I said sarcastically, trying to squirm out of his grasp.

Then Jimmy's voice appeared from behind. "What's going on?"

"Heeeere's Jimmy! Da da da da da…" David sung to himself and then doubled over with laughter from his own joke. Jimmy also thought the whole thing was very funny.

"Thank you David, for having me on the show!" Jimmy said. I gave him a you-are-insane look.

"Pleasure. Pleasure," David said, holding in his giggles.

"And now, for my next act, with the help of my lovely assistant, I will perform a very dangerous magic trick." Jimmy began. My mouth flew open. David was on cloud nine and Amanda looked somewhat amused.

"But you have to close your eyes," Jimmy added.

"Oh come on!" David said.

"Yes, yes. Keep them closed," Jimmy instructed.

"No way!" David protested. Amanda kept quiet but was game. Her eyes were shut.

"You won't be sorry," Jimmy said. Finally, David closed his eyes.

"Keep them closed," said Jimmy. "Okay. Count to thirty!"

Jimmy grabbed my hand and led me down the hallway. With a few giggles escaping my mouth, we managed to tiptoe away without anyone knowing.

"Shhh!" he said when we were halfway down the next wing of the school.

"Thanks," I said as we reached the library. I was half relieved, half confused, and a hundred percent totally peeved at the same time. ;)

Just before the lunch bell rang, I was on the floor, on my hands and knees, trying to find my math notebook, which was somewhere in the back corner of my locker. I'd probably put it there on purpose, a subconscious wish. Amanda's voice appeared.

"Did you hear what I told you?"

Half of my body was still in my locker as I said: "Yes."

"Well?"

I got up, with my found spiral notebook in hand. I could feel my eyebrows scrunched up from confusion.

She stared at me.

The bell rang, so I shook my head and walked away to my next class.

Mr. Drane was at his desk, shuffling through the math textbook, just like he always did before class. I stood before him and announced, quietly:

"A Martian approached me from Pluto, but I will ignore her and return to planet Earth."

He smiled. I took my seat.

But it was hard, very hard to put Amanda, the Martian, out of my head so that I could concentrate on what Mr. Drane was explaining. I had to, though, because my grades depended on it. I vowed to myself to go to his math clinic the following day.

"Amanda told me that her parents are getting a divorce, and David thinks my ass is hot," I announced in Marna's office later that afternoon.

"Wow."

"Yeah."

"Okay, let's start with the first piece of news."

"Okay."

"Why do you think Amanda told you this?"

"I don't know."

"Yes, you do."

"If I knew, I would tell you, wouldn't I?" I said impatiently.

"Just try and answer the question."

I sat and thought. I took a deep breath.

"Okay, let me help you," Marna offered.

"That would be nice," I said impatiently.

"Let's go back to the time when you were friends."

"Right."

"Who did Amanda talk to when she failed a test?"

"Me."

"Got dumped?"

"Me."

"Why?"

"Well, I remember the time when Amanda got dumped by this guy who was in grade ten. We were in grade eight. He broke up with her for no reason. Probably knew he wouldn't get 'it' from her. Anyways, she was so upset, she cried and cried for days. She would call Lisa, Gail, and me, and we would hear nothing but her sniffling and the blowing of her nose. Gail and Lisa told me they thought she'd lost her marbles. I...I don't know. It didn't bother me as much. She was upset and she was my friend, so I just listened."

"Uh-huh."

Marna just looked at me.

"Oh," I said, when it dawned on me.

"Yeah," Marna said. "She needs you now, regardless of what happened in the past."

"Well, why should I listen to her now?"

"Is that your decision?"

"What do you mean, 'my decision'? What kind of a lowlife would be sympathetic to Amanda after what she did to me?"

"It's called forgiveness."

"Me, forgive her? No way."

"Just think about it."

"What's to think?" I asked, insulted. "And," I continued, changing the subject, "what about David's comment?"

"What do you think about it?"

"Oh, never mind," I said, laughing, realizing that it was a compliment even though it was from a pig like David.

When I came home that evening, I threw my school bag on the floor and flung my jacket into the air. It ended up hitting the chandelier. Cling clang, it chimed loudly.

"Elizabeth!" my mother yelled, walking briskly into the front hallway from the kitchen. She tended to call me by my full name whenever she was annoyed—and indeed she was.

"Sorry, mom," I said.

"We do not throw our things on the floor—or in the air—in this house," she said sternly.

Silence.

"Dinner won't be ready for another forty-five minutes or so," she said.

"Good. I need to go for a run."

My mother nodded and went back to the kitchen.

I quickly changed out of my school clothes and into my winter jogging outfit that I had bought the previous week. This included the special winter "tracks" that attached to my sneakers so that I would have less of a chance of slipping on the ice and falling on my rear end. The cold air felt great on my face, as did each cold breath I inhaled. I ran faster and faster, my arms swinging fiercely back and forth as my knees went higher and higher. I didn't need my iPod on this run because my frustration was my music. For each step I ran, I pictured Amanda's two faces. Her sad one, caused by her parents, and her mischievous one, caused by each prank or mean comment that she conjured. Lisa and Gail's oblivious behaviour also entered my mind. I wondered if they cared that Amanda wanted me instead of them to talk to. They didn't seem to care, last time I checked. I also thought about Jimmy "saving" me the other day in the cafeteria. I didn't need saving. I could have handled them on my own. I shook my head as I continued to run.

After four blocks, I turned around and came home. I peeked into the kitchen, and my mother informed me that I had just enough time to take a shower before dinner would be on the table.

When I emerged from the bathroom, wearing my bathrobe, my mother was waiting for me in my bedroom.

"Amanda called while you were in the shower."

"Nng."

"Why is she calling you?"

"Her parents are splitting up."

"That's terrible. But why is she telling you this? Doesn't she have other friends that she doesn't treat like yesterday's garbage?"

"Yes, she does, but apparently she doesn't want them. She wants me."

"Can't blame her," my mother nodded. "Are you going to call her back?"

"Don't know. All I want to do right now is eat dinner. I'm starving," I said as I quickly changed into sweat pants and a T-shirt.

I didn't end up calling Amanda back that night. I wasn't ready. I just wasn't prepared to talk to her yet.

Chapter 29

A few days later at lunch, I was in Mr. Drane's office, trying to understand a word problem. I had that weird and confused look on my face again.

"How's Pluto?" he asked, looking frustrated.

"Pluto's for putzes!" I exclaimed.

"Go on," he said as he walked away from the chalkboard. I started to fill him on the latest scoop.

"How does Amanda expect me to talk to her?" I asked rhetorically.

"'To err is human; to forgive, divine': Alexander Pope," he said.

"Pope schmope!" I said.

There was a knock at the door. David poked his head in.

"Hey, come on in," Mr. Drane said.

I looked at Mr. Drane as if he'd taken my teddy bear away.

"Lizzie, you know David."

I faked a smile.

"I don't get this," David said as he motioned to the chalkboard.

I nodded.

"Hey," Mr. Drane said when he noticed my response to David's presence, "this math clinic is available to everyone."

"I know," I said, looking down at my notebook.

David and I spent the next half hour in silence as Mr. Drane went over the material. I didn't look at David once, but I knew he was looking at me. When the bell rang, we collected our books and I made a mad dash to the door. I tended to do that when David was around.

"Lizzie!" David yelled, when I was almost halfway down the hallway. I stopped.

"I'm sorry," he said.

I walked back towards him and looked him in the eye.

"Sorry for what?"

"Being an ass."

I looked at him as he looked down at the floor.

"Jimmy's a lucky guy," he said shyly.

I smiled. "Just quit swinging me around. It's really annoying."

"But it's fun," he laughed.

"Not for me."

"Okay," he said, looking at the floor.

"Okay."

David swinging me around may have been only a small part of my problems, but it was a start. The bigger problem was Lisa, Amanda, and Gail, who I couldn't figure out. I didn't even know if they cared whether I existed.

It turned out that they did care, but not in a good way. A little while later at home, after Lee had tried and failed to convince me to go for a run, I was trying to figure my math homework out by myself. The phone rang.

"We could have emailed you, but we wanted to ask you this in person," Lisa announced.

"What do you mean, 'we?'" I asked. My eyes were crinkled like yesterday's newspaper.

"What's with you and David?" Gail asked.

"I told him to stop swinging me around. I was getting nauseous."

"That's it?" Lisa asked.

"Yup," I said.

"So, what gives?" Gail asked.

"What?" I asked.

"He's our friend," Lisa said.

"Okay," I said, confused.

"So one guy is not enough for you? Do you like him too, now?"

"Oh my G-d. This is crazy," I declared. "Like I said, all I did was ask him to stop swinging me around the hallway. That's it. Finito!"

"Sure," Lisa hissed.

I hung up the phone feeling completely ridiculous and unbelievably annoyed. I couldn't understand how or why they were treating me this way.

I stared at my math books once again, so I could think about something more logical. Then the phone rang again.

"Hello," Jimmy's sweet voice said.

"Can't do it. Too hard."

"What, hold the telephone in your hand?"

"No…" I paused, then decided to continue. "Gail and Lisa just gave me a hard time about David. They think I like him or something. But all

I did was ask him to stop swinging me around."

"Well, it's about time. I mean, he physically abuses you!"

"Well, he's gonna stop now," I asserted.

"He probably wants you," Jimmy suggested.

"I don't want him! I just wanted him to stop smashing my body into lockers!"

"If you need me to…" Jimmy began, but I cut him right off.

"Enough with the Prince Charming act, okay? I can take care of myself."

"Okay, Joan of Arc," he said snidely.

"Will you cut that out?"

"Why are you being so touchy?"

"Touchy? Look, maybe we should take a break from touching each other." I couldn't believe that came out of my mouth, but I was feeling suffocated and I needed space.

"What are you saying?"

"I just need to be alone right now, and figure a few things out."

"Great, go figure some things out with David." He hung up.

I stared at the phone. My hand was still on the receiver; I was gripping it as hard as I could, and I couldn't let go.

I couldn't believe that I had just broken up with him. My eyes darted around my bedroom as I tried to put the roller coaster of the last thirty minutes into perspective. Lisa and Gail harass me, my boyfriend gets annoyed, and I break up with him.

I took a deep breath then got up from my bed and walked into the kitchen. Lee was making a milkshake. His eyes greeted mine.

"What's wrong?" he asked.

"Jimmy and I broke up."

"What?"

"Yep."

"When?"

"Five minutes ago."

"Why?"

I tensed up my shoulders.

"He's too over-protective. He didn't like the fact that I told David to stop swinging me around or that I can take care of myself."

"That's it?" he asked.

"Yeah, that's it," I said, sighing.

Lee took a deep breath and then let it out.

"You are a nut case!" he yelled.

"Excuse me?" I yelled back.

"So what if he's a little over-protective? He's just looking out for you! Why the hell can you forgive a guy who mistook you for a trapeze artist but not forgive Jimmy for caring?"

That did it. I wanted to shake him. Why couldn't he understand me? This was all getting too complicated. I put my hands over my face and started to cry.

"Oh, don't get all PMS on me now. I got enough of that from Linda all last week."

My mother came into the kitchen.

"What is going on?"

"Lizzie, are you breathing okay?" she asked. "Should I get a paper bag?" She had a panicked look on her face.

"No, Mom, I'm not having a panic attack," I said through sobs.

The doorbell rang and I ran to my room, shut the door, and sat down in a corner near my humungous pink stuffed dog. I heard a knock.

"Yes?" I said through tears.

"Can I come in?" Jimmy said through the door.

I got up and opened the door. His face fell as soon as he saw me. I walked back to my corner and he kneeled down to talk to me.

"Look, I don't know what happened there," he said.

I stared at the floor.

"You can be friends with whomever you want," he said.

"I know. I just need my space right now." I looked up at him.

"I'll give you space."

"Listen to me. I need to figure a few things out. I don't know who I am, who my friends are, or if I am going to get by this year in math."

"I can help you in math!"

"No you can't!" I yelled.

It startled him.

"I just don't want to have a boyfriend right now," I whispered.

He took a deep breath, got up, and left. I waited five minutes for Jimmy to say goodbye to my parents. Then I got up, went over to my desk where my math books were, and threw them across the room. They knocked over a picture of Lisa, Amanda, Gail, and me that I still had on my shelf. Funny, I didn't remember having aimed the math books in that direction.

* * *

"Why did you do it?" Marna asked the following day.

"There you go with those questions again," I said impatiently.

"Why?" she asked again.

"Because I need to figure a few things out!"

"What kind of things?"

"What were you doing while I was spilling my guts out to you for the past two months, picking your nose?" I asked.

Marna was silent. Perhaps she didn't appreciate my sarcasm.

"Math, myself, LAG…" I offered.

"What about them?"

"I hate them."

"Why?"

"Like I said before, where were you these past two months?"

"Yes," she said calmly. "I know what happened. But how does it all make you feel?"

"Well, I might as well start in chronological order," I said. "The party in October? On an embarrassment scale of one to ten, it was about a seventy-four. The rumour that I had sex with Jimmy in the bathroom at the party: I felt betrayed like a character in a soap opera plot. The reading of my diary on the intercom: Well, that one takes the cake. I think I would rather run naked in front of the school."

Marna stared at me and crossed her arms.

"Tell me about you and Amanda, last year at this time."

"I already told you a story last session. You know the one about the guy she liked in grade ten?"

"I know," she said. "I like hearing these stories. There must be more."

Feeling frustrated, but willing to play along—because by that point, I was hoping that Marna had a purpose to her questions—I searched my memory back to March of the previous year.

"Okay, let's see. Oh yeah. It was Purim, and since we belong to the same synagogue, we both volunteered to help out with the party to get extra credit. Amanda had this huge crush on one of the other volunteers, and she made such a spectacle of herself. It was really embarrassing."

"What did she do?"

"She would wear these really revealing outfits and always ask for help when there was something that she had to lift. 'Oh Gary!'—that was his name—'Can you help me lift this bag of sugar cubes?' she would say, in a helpless voice."

"What did you do?"

"I took her aside and said to try and not be so obvious, to play a little hard to get. I gave her some examples, but she didn't get it."

Marna smiled.

"Put it this way: by the time the party came around, Gary was playing Pin the Tail on Haman with another girl.

"And what did you guys do?"

"I wanted to get her mind off of being rejected, so I gathered her and a bunch of other volunteers and we danced the rest of the night. We had a blast."

"She was lucky to have you by her side."

"Yeah, I really looked out for her, and I remember feeling good about it. I still feel good about it. Oh geez."

Marna smiled.

"You must love this," I said.

"You don't know how much," she said, smiling.

"Okay, two things are happening here: First of all, I am beginning to feel sorry for Amanda, and second of all, I'm realizing that maybe it's okay for someone like Jimmy to look out for me, just like I looked out for Amanda last year. But I don't know; I need more time to think about Jimmy. Can I just talk about Amanda right now?"

"You can talk about anything you like."

"Okay... Maybe a tiny, weeny part of me broke up with Jimmy because Amanda liked him first back in September."

Marna was smiling and nodding.

"But why did I not have these feelings when I first met Jimmy and wanted to date him? Why now?"

"Back then she was bugging you, teasing you. You were probably sick of it and subconsciously wanted to get her back by going out with Jimmy."

"Oh my gosh," I said. "You just gave me a freebie!"

"You deserve it. You had a big breakthrough today," she said.

"I'd say a beautiful relationship developed between you and Jimmy because of all of this," she continued. "You have to decide if you want to continue it. For you," she stressed, looking in my eyes. "Not for Amanda; not for anyone but you."

"Can't you give me one more freebie?" I asked coyly.

"Only one per customer!" Marna smiled.

Chapter 30

The next week at school, I spent all of my lunch hours at Mr. Drane's math clinic because the bathroom stalls became too stinky to eat in. Plus, I was more motivated than ever to pass math.

I officially had no real friends anymore. Yes, there was David, and he joined me with Mr. Drane at lunch a few times. But just because we were on speaking terms didn't mean I was going to hang out with him. Besides, it was March, and since the weather had warmed up, David was spending more time outside with the rest of the jocks.

One Friday, I was relieved to discover that my parents were going to the country. I couldn't bear another weekend alone in my room.

"I'm coming with you," I said when they got home from work and were taking off their coats.

"But Lee wants to take you to that new James Bond movie, and the Goldbergs won't be there because they're touring with Jenny, so it'll be kinda boring for you," my mother told me.

"Don't care. I need a change of environment. Plus, I want to ski."

I went to my bedroom to pack.

At the ski hill on Saturday morning while I was in line to buy a ticket I saw a vision. My eyes opened wide and I took a deep breath. I said aloud: "It couldn't be…"

But it was. Sam Green. I was so happy to see him—it had been a while since I'd had any real contact with someone close to my age, and I decided that right now he would be the perfect companion. I approached him from behind by tapping him gently on the shoulder. I was relieved to see his smile was as bright as mine when we saw each other. "What a bonus for my spring break!" he said. We skied together for a few runs, and then he casually informed me that he broke up with his girlfriend at school. "Aww… I'm so sorry," I said as sad as I could while I was jumping for joy inside. Then, he put forth the most exciting proposition:

"Ever see *Dial M for Murder* by Alfred Hitchcock?"

I shook my head.

"Pop some popcorn. I'll be over at eight."

It was if he had hypnotized me and I was in a trance. I stared straight ahead and nodded with a smile that grew as the day went on. I couldn't believe this was happening. I felt a slight twinge of guilt since I had just broken up with Jimmy, but not guilty enough to pass up this offer!

When I got home I was so excited I couldn't see straight. I didn't know if I should shower first, or pop the popcorn, or pick out my clothes, or choose which colour eyeliner to use. I was running around in circles until my mother stopped me and asked what was going on.

"Sam Green is coming over to watch a movie!" I shrieked.

"THE Sam Green?" she asked.

"Yes!" I said impatiently.

My mother's eyes glazed over. "I remember my Sam Green… Bobby Linger," she said. "Oh, he was sooooo cute. I was sixteen and he was seventeen…" she went off into another world.

"Oh, Mom!" I yelled. "Not now!"

"He came over to watch movies too," she said. Then she gave me a look of concern. "And we watched them, you know."

"Sure you did," my dad piped in.

I peeled off my ski clothes and ran into the bathroom to shower. As I stood with my sopping wet hair (which started to curl and frizz the moment it hit dry air), I decided that this would not be a good time to straighten it, even though HE was coming over. My excitement was making me fidgety, so I reached for my gel and anti-frizz serum and went for the natural look.

Then I stared at my weekend bag. All I had were sweats. "I didn't know this was going to happen!" I whined aloud to myself. I looked around the room and noticed a pair of jeans in the closet. Apparently Linda had forgotten her jeans the last time she was here. I decided to try them on. I slipped them up my legs and over my hips. I couldn't believe that they fit. Then I looked at myself in the mirror and a huge grin grew across my face. *This is good*, I thought. *Really good.*

I brushed my teeth, and put on a little blush, mascara, and lip gloss.

"Dinner, Lizzie!" my mom yelled from the kitchen.

"Dinner? How could I eat at a time like this?" I yelled.

"Well, at least have some chicken noodle soup," she yelled back. "Come on, it's your favourite!"

I agreed that it would be a good idea. I went downstairs and slurped whatever I could manage while my heart pounded a mile a minute.

"Just to let you know, the Cranbergs are coming over for cocktails. So we will be home," my dad warned.

"That's fine," I said in my sweet, obedient voice. I would be damned if I was going to piss them off at this point.

Eight o'clock came and went. I stared at the clock in disbelief. *What happens if he doesn't show?* Well, at least I hadn't straightened my hair. That would have been a real waste.

At 8:30, the doorbell rang. It was the Cranbergs…with Sam right behind them.

"Well, look who we found in your driveway, Sweetie Lizzie," said Mrs. Cranberg. I hated when the Cranbergs called me that. I faked a grin.

"Who?" I asked, gamely.

"Your date!" Mr. Cranberg said. I thought I was going to faint from complete embarrassment.

"Hi, date!" Sam joked.

"Hi," I said, grabbing his hand to lead him into the basement, where we were going to watch the movie.

Sam looked too good for words. Wearing jeans and a sweatshirt, he looked like one of those models from Abercrombie and Fitch, the sexy, mildly obscene clothing catalogue that I wasn't allowed to look at until I turned fourteen. With holes in his jeans and his collarbones showing through his sweatshirt, he was the epitome of sexiness, and I wanted to be a part of it. After we chatted for a while about school and stuff, I went upstairs to get the popcorn and drinks while he set up the movie.

"Don't set off the smoke alarm down there!" Mr. Cranberg joked from the peanut gallery.

"Very funny," I said tersely.

When I came back downstairs Sam said, "Lizzie, you look very good."

My heart started to pound like the drummer from the rock band KISS.

"I started jogging," I said in a shaky voice.

He put his arm around me and ran his hands through my hair. I prayed that it wasn't going to get caught in my nest. It didn't.

He leaned over and gently pressed his lips to mine. I fell into his grasp and surrendered myself to his lead. I couldn't believe this was happening, and my mind began to wander. Immediately, Jimmy's face appeared in my mind, along with his touch and the scent of his body. I pulled away from Sam. I smiled. "Let's watch the movie," I said. *What was I, a complete idiot?*

We watched the movie, but I didn't pay attention. How could I? My mind was bouncing back from Jimmy to Sam like a Ping-Pong tournament.

After the movie, we talked for a little while, and then Sam wanted to head home. He wanted to ski a couple of runs in the morning before his train left for school.

"You're a cool chick, Liz. I'll call you when I get back to school. I tend to come in from time to time."

"Great," I said politely.

He put on his jacket, slipped on his boots, gave me a kiss on the cheek, and left. I watched him through our front door window as he got in his car and drove off.

Chapter 31

On Sunday afternoon, on our way home to the city, I sat in the back seat of my dad's car, staring into space and fiddling with the seatbelt button. I was making a great clicking sound.

My mom turned around to give me an annoyed look.

"Mmm?" I asked, still clicking.

"Can you just put on your seatbelt and not play with it?"

"Wha? Oh yeah, sure," I said.

Click, click, click.

"Lizzie!" my dad yelled.

"Sorry," I said, startled. "I forgot."

"What's going on?" my mom asked.

"Nothing," I said softly.

"Oh yeah, sure," she said. "Sam Green nothing." She turned around to smile at me. I didn't smile, but just stared straight ahead.

I should have been on cloud nine, but strangely enough I wasn't. Last night I locked lips with a guy I've had a crush on since as long as I can remember, and instead of celebrating my daydreams coming true, all I felt was, well, weird. I shook my head as I thought about it. Sam was beautiful in every way. Why did I feel so weird?

Click, click, click.

"Elizabeth! Put on your iPod!" my mother yelled.

It was the kiss. The kiss was like a dream, almost imaginary. But there was no comparison between Sam's imaginary and Jimmy's real and intense feeling.

I went to bed that night holding Jimmy's socks to my chest. Yes, I still had them. I missed being with him. I missed his soft cottony rugby shirts and the way they smelled when I buried my face into his shoulder when I hugged him. I felt I needed him, but I wasn't sure if I should get back together with him. Then I thought about giving Sam a call. Maybe if I kissed him a second time it wouldn't be as imaginary—it would become real. I tossed and turned both ideas around in my head until I could hear the birds chirp the next morning.

It was a miracle that I got myself to school. I didn't think I'd slept for even an hour in total.

As I stumbled into class and sat at my desk, I plunked my head into my hands to close my eyes, for just a second.

"Hey!" a voice said.

"Lizzie!" another voice said.

"Hey—wake up!" David said, with a gentle nudge.

"Wha? Oh my G-d." I popped up my head and started looking frantically all around.

"You look like crap," David said.

"Give me a break," I said, rubbing my eyes. "I didn't sleep a wink last night."

"Next time, get some more shut-eye," he said.

"What's going on?" I said, stretching.

"We just got our partners for an English presentation," David explained.

I yawned. "Oh cool. Who am I with?"

"Me," Gail's voice said from behind my chair.

I quickly spun around to meet her face.

"You?"

"Yep," she said sardonically. "Look, I already put a request in to work with someone else."

"Lisa, no doubt?" I said.

"Yes, but it's not happening. You're stuck with me."

"Oh goodie."

"David, can Gail sit in your seat?" I asked.

"What, no catfight?" he asked, smiling.

I clenched my teeth and gave David an annoyed look.

And on he moved. Gail sat down and, believe it or not, we put our feelings towards one another outside the classroom door and worked. Actually, we didn't entirely work together. First, we went to opposite ends of the classroom with our notebooks and brainstormed ideas on what to present. I made sure my part was very detailed because the less I had to work with her the better. During the last fifteen minutes of the class we shared our ideas and decided on a topic and plan of action.

Then the bell rang.

"Wait—we have to meet again to finish," I said.

She made a sour face.

"Look, this is for thirty percent of our final mark. And because of math, my GPA is on the line."

She sighed. "Free Saturday?" she asked.

"Hold on," I said. "Let me think."

I paused, and Gail looked confused. She must have been surprised by the idea that I could possibly have other plans.

"Yeah, I'm free," I said finally. "How about my house at 7:00?"

* * *

As the rest of the week went by, I caught up on my sleep by going to bed by 8:30 almost every night. What purpose was there staying up? Who was I going to iChat/email/text with? Plus, I had no patience for TV. I spent my lunch hour with Mr. Drane and David (since it rained most of the week), and spoke approximately ten times to Lisa and Gail, each conversation consisting of "Hi" and "Bye" and nothing else. Oh, yes, there was one bonus: "See you on Saturday," said Gail on Friday afternoon.

But then of course, there was Jimmy.

I saw him once on Monday.

Twice on Tuesday.

Five times on Wednesday.

Twice on Thursday.

On Friday, I didn't see him. He was on a field trip.

Whenever I did see him that week, I would stop, stare at him, and try to smile, but the corners of my mouth couldn't seem to turn up. My stomach would be all in knots, and I could feel my pulse racking violently through my body. It sounded crazy, but even though I had broken up with him, I felt like I had cheated on him with Sam. I was confused, and so was he. I could tell because whenever we saw each other, his mouth would open up as if he was going to say something, but no words came out.

Saturday evening arrived. My parents were in the country, so it was just Lee and me at home. It was 6:30 and I was in the kitchen making popcorn on the stove.

"Uh, we have the microwave kind in the pantry," Lee said.

"Duh," I said. "I know. This way is healthier. Less chemicals. I've got some olive oil in here."

Lee laughed. "I'll say it one more time: I've created a monster."

I smiled a toothy grin.

"And who could be deserving of this healthy treat, since Jimmy flew the coop?" Lee asked, sampling my popcorn.

"Gail," I said, dumping it into a bowl.

"Gail Gail?" Lee was incredulous.

"Yep."

I explained to him my sleepless night and rude awakening the previous Monday morning. Lee was in shock. Especially about the Sam part—but I was saved from getting into that can of worms when the doorbell rang. Lee went to answer it. My heart skipped a beat. I had to admit that I was a bit nervous about being alone with Gail.

It was Linda.

"Why is Gail coming over?" she asked as she walked into the kitchen.

"News travels fast," I said.

The doorbell rang again.

"I'll get it." I ran to the front door.

This time it was Gail. I brought her into the kitchen, and Lee and Linda stared at her as though they were trying to burn a hole through her clothes with their eyes.

"Okay guys," I said. "Gail and I have to work on our English thing. Don't you have a frat party to go to?"

"It doesn't start for another three hours," Linda said, firing daggers through Gail's jeans.

"Well, go have dinner first or something," I ordered.

"Okay," Lee said, getting the hint, and he took Linda's hand and left the kitchen.

Gail looked bothered.

"They're just looking out for me," I said.

Gail nodded.

In the first five minutes her cell phone rang twice. The first call was from her brother (he wanted a phone number), and the second call was from Lisa. They didn't talk long. I was impressed. I took out my binder and laid it on the kitchen table. I kept my head lowered while I read, avoiding Gail's eyes.

"What are you reading?" Gail asked.

"My notes from class."

"Well, why?"

"To prepare for this assignment," I said, stating the obvious. "Why are you acting so weird?"

"Look," she said smugly. "I know what I'm doing."

"Do you?"

"I know those characters like the back of my hand."

Just like you knew me, I thought.

"I know what it takes to get an A."

Just like you know what I need, I thought.

I stared at her.

"Hello?" Gail waved her hands in front of my face.

I snapped out of my trance.

"Uh, yeah. Okay, look. Let's just memorize what we wrote down in class the other day and we'll be fine."

"Duh," she said. "I don't even know why we had this meeting in the first place."

"Well, I just like to be prepared," I said. Then I decided to take action and get it over with. "Fine. Let's write down exactly what we are going to say," I announced as I opened my laptop, began a new folder, and started to type away. Then when we were done, we rehearsed twice.

"We should be fine," I said as we waited for Gail's mom to pick her up.

"Yeah, we worked well," she agreed.

I wanted to say more. A whole bunch of things. But before I could say anything, a honk was heard and Gail was out the door.

On Sunday, I decided to call her.

"Hi," I began.

"Hi."

"What happened to us?"

"I don't know."

"Maybe it was fate that we got put together for this assignment."

"Maybe."

"You okay?" I asked.

"Yeah."

"We'll do great tomorrow."

"Uh-huh."

"See you tomorrow."

I hung up the phone and realized that I had tried to crack open an egg but there was nothing inside. Little did I know that an extra large Mexican omelette would be waiting for me on Monday morning.

Chapter 32

As I opened my locker to take off my coat and collect my books, Gail and Lisa came up to me, smiling.

"Hi guys," I said, smiling back.

"Can't wait to see what you and Gail stirred up," Lisa said.

"Yeah, we did a pretty good job on Saturday night," I said looking at Gail.

The three of us walked into class together, and it felt like I was being taken to a spaceship by two aliens.

David and Lisa were paired together, and went first. As I was trying to go over my lines, a text message appeared on my cell phone, and I responded right away.

Gail: Don't feel like listening. Let's talk.

My stomach turned upside down.

ME: Why now?

GAIL: You know.

Me: No, I don't.

Gail: Yes, you do.

Me: Don't get it. Stop this. Not before we go up.

Gail: Let's just get it out in the open right now.

Me: Oh come on!

Gail: Let's have a clear conscience!

Me: What do you think this is, confession?

I shut my cell phone.

Our names were called.

At the front of the class, I began to speak:

"*Of Mice and Men* is a story about two men and their strong bond of friendship, protection, and loyalty for one another."

"Friendship, protection, and loyalty," I repeated as I scanned the classroom and found Lisa and Amanda staring at me. My heart began to beat faster, and I felt a droplet of sweat run down my neck.

"A character named Crooks…" I began, but then I trailed off and started to breathe heavily and feel dizzy. Oh no, I thought—another panic attack. Not now. I walked over to my backpack and grabbed my water bottle.

"Are you okay?" my teacher asked as I gulped. I nodded.

Gail took over, but I didn't pay attention to anything she said. My mind was in a time machine, traveling to a moment from elementary school when Gail and I were watching *Gilligan's Island*, then jumping to images of having heart-to-heart talks with Lisa. It jumped to memories of listening to Amanda's boyfriend woes, of watching them smoke, of feeling completely alone, of eating my lunch on a toilet flusher. All these scenes were spinning around in my head, and I wanted it to stop so I could finish my presentation.

"Wait!" I blurted out.

Gail's eyes were glaring.

"Why did you spread a rumour that I had sex with Jimmy, and why did you read my diary on the school intercom!"

The whole class started talking. My teacher's eyes grew larger, but she didn't say anything. Everyone was whispering and waiting for my next move.

"You just don't do that to a person," I said, "to a friend."

Gail was shaking.

"Why?"

Gail didn't answer.

"Do you need your Olsen Twin to help you answer?"

"Amanda liked Jimmy," Lisa yelled from her desk. "You took him away from her!"

"Hey," I said. "That's between me and Amanda."

"Yeah, Lisa," Amanda said.

"We can handle this, Amanda!" Lisa yelled.

"No you can't!" Amanda yelled back.

I looked at Amanda. I was in total shock. So was she.

"I didn't take your diary," Gail said.

"Who did?" I barked.

"I did," said David.

"You?" I asked, completely shocked.

"I'm sorry. It was really cool poetry, and I wanted everyone to hear it."

"How did you get it?" I asked.

"Went into your room when you weren't home. Your cleaning lady let me in. I told her I'd forgotten a sweatshirt in your room."

"I don't believe this!" I said, raising my hands in the air. "Why did you drag my life through hell? All of you? Do you know how many times I ate my lunch on the fucking toilet?"

"Lizzie Stein! Go to the office, now!" my teacher yelled. I didn't blame her.

"What you all did was unforgivable," I continued.

"Lizzie. Go. Now."

"You forgave David," Gail said.

"That is my business, not yours," I said.

The whole class sat motionless. My teacher pointed her finger towards the door, and I took my books and left.

Chapter 33

My sweaty palms gripped the sides of my seat as I sat in The Row: a line of chairs that faced the front desk in the school office. In our school, it was the equivalent of death row. You were in deep, big trouble if you found yourself in one of those seats, facing the secretary as she typed away at her computer and threw dirty looks at you every so often.

I looked to my right and my left to greet my fellow offenders.

There was Lina White with her ever-changing hair colour and multitude of body piercings. I smiled as I looked at her but kept my gaze short due to the fact that she had a habit of being overly suspicious for no apparent reason. And then, out of the corner of my eye, I saw Ian Capinsky sitting on the far end of The Row, leaning on the windowsill. He had a habit of throwing chairs as high as he could into the air whenever he got upset. He was a strong guy, and I wondered if David could match that circus act. I didn't dare look Ian in the eye. I was in no mood to be on the lookout for falling chairs.

And then there was me. Lizzie Stein, who'd never been in trouble like this before. Sure, I got yelled at for giggling too much or passing notes. But this was my first time on The Row.

"What you in for?" Lina asked.

Shocked by her comment, but wanting to stay cool at the same time, I filled her in on the events of the last ten minutes.

"Oh, cool," she said, nodding. I smiled.

Finally, Mr. Chow called my name. I got up to face the music.

"And to what do I owe this visit, Ms. Stein?" he asked.

"I kind of freaked out," I said.

"Well, either you tell me everything now, or I will ask Ms. Green."

I told him. Everything. And I mean everything. From my early sense that things were weird when I got home from camp, to the ugly rumour about Jimmy, to my panic attack (which he recalled), to eating my lunch on a toilet (which he thought was disgusting), to my panic about failing math, to the stealing of my diary, and the reading of a poem from it on the intercom.

He recalled the intercom incident, and apologized.

"Uh, yeah," I said. "How exactly did you let that one happen?"

"They were supposed to read poetry from a published author," Mr. Chow explained. "I wasn't expecting it to be an excerpt from your diary."

"Oh," I said, looking at the floor.

I continued to tell him that after all of that, Amanda needed my friendship because her parents were splitting up. I told him that Gail and Lisa were pissing me off even more.

"Wow," he said.

"Yup," I said.

"I see you have a lot on your plate."

"Thanks," I said, and I really meant it, because it felt great to have a principal who actually cared and wasn't out to punish me.

"But that doesn't mean that I'm letting you off the hook."

Wishful thinking.

"Can I pick my punishment?" I asked.

"Pardon me?" he asked, raising his eyeglasses to his forehead.

"I just thought I'd try," I said. "At this point, what do I have to lose?"

"Alright," he said gamely.

"I can come to detention for a week, in the morning," I announced.

"What's your hidden agenda?"

"I need time for math. Mr. Drane holds a lunchtime clinic and I go often, but I need to go more. I know he has one at 7:00 am."

"Make it two weeks, and you've got a deal."

I got up, we shook hands, and I left, beaming. "Who put extra sugar in your Corn Flakes this morning?" Ian said as I was leaving.

"Me."

* * *

The next morning, I awoke at the ghastly hour of 6:00. I was on the bus by 6:30 and at school by 7:00.

I knocked on Mr. Drane's door.

"Yes?" said Mr. Drane.

"Surprise! I got detention for two weeks!"

"I heard. Mazel Tov."

"Thanks," I said as I walked into the classroom. I noticed another girl sitting at a nearby desk. I knew she was in the grade ahead of me, and I'd seen her around in the halls. Mr. Drane introduced us. Her name was Stephanie.

"You go to my synagogue," she said.

"I do?"

"I sit up close to the mechitza."

I stared at her and tried to recall the very little time I had spent in the synagogue sanctuary—since I tended to spend the majority of my time there in the girls' bathroom.

"Have a seat," she said.

"Thanks," I said shyly, opening my books.

While Stephanie tried some parabolas, Mr. Drane and I tried to decode a few problem-solving questions.

"I hate these," I said under my breath.

"I hated those last year," Stephanie said, erasing, for the third time, a question she'd been working on.

* * *

"Do you come every day?" I asked Stephanie the next morning as we were unpacking our school bags. Mr. Drane was getting milk for his coffee in the staff lounge.

"Just about."

"Math isn't really my thing."

"Mine neither."

"They should make it an elective."

"Totally."

"Why don't you come at lunch time?" I asked her.

234

"Because by the time I've finished eating, I have to say a few prayers, and then there's no time for me to hang out with my friends. I just want lunchtime to be relaxing. And math is not relaxing."

I smiled in agreement.

"Don't you miss hanging out with your friends?" she asked.

"Not really. I'm kind of in between friends now."

"Oh."

Mr. Drane came back to the classroom and shared his special Colombian roast with Stephanie and me.

When the first-period bell rang, Jimmy was standing by the door waiting for me.

"How are you?" he asked.

"Fine," I said.

"How's your math coming along?"

"Okay, I guess."

After a few moments of awkward silence, I walked away.

Later on in the evening, while I was on my bed reading a magazine, the phone rang. It was Sam.

"How are you?" he asked.

"Fine," I said in a monotone voice.

Strange coincidence. But Sam was more persistent than Jimmy was.

"That's all you can say?"

"Yep."

"I'm coming into town this weekend and I'd really like to see you."

I couldn't take the pressure, the temptation, or the confusion.

"I'm just going through a lot of stuff right now," I blurted out. "This may seem crazy, but even though I'd like to see you, I can't. My heart wouldn't be in it."

"Why? I thought we had a great time together."

"We did."

"Then?"

"I don't know. Just leave it at that."

I hung up.

The next morning, in between math problems, Stephanie looked over at my paper and corrected a mistake I had made.

"Thanks," I said. "I keep forgetting that step."

"I made the same mistake last year on my final. Hated that."

I nodded.

"Hey, there's a Purim party at the synagogue this weekend."

"I volunteered for that party last year for extra credit," I said. "It was fun and all, but I don't need the volunteer credit for this year."

"I'm not asking you to work, but to be a guest."

"Oh, I'm not into that stuff," I admitted. "I only go to synagogue on high holidays."

"Come on, it'll be fun."

"Nah," I said. "Not for me. But thanks."

"Oh, come on," Stephanie persisted.

"You should go, Lizzie," Mr. Drane intervened.

"What else do you have to do?" Stephanie asked teasingly.

"You do have a point," I said.

Chapter 34

That Saturday night, I stood in front of my closet wrapped in a towel, looking for a costume. I felt cold droplets of water splash on my shoulders from my hair. I let out a huge sigh. I didn't know why I was standing there; there were no costumes in my closet, only clothes.

My mother poked her head into my bedroom. My parents were in town that weekend, because the only thing left up north was mud.

"What were you thinking of dressing up as?"

"Dunno."

"I may have something," she said suggestively, in her chipper tone. She came back with an Indian sari.

"You've got to be kidding," I said.

"Oh come on, try it. It'll look great on you," she said. "And I'll help you straighten your haaa-aair!" she sang.

Those were the magic words.

On went the sari (which didn't look as hideous as I'd feared), and on went the blow-dryer. My mother's strong arms worked their way through my annoyingly frizzy curls, and to seal the deal she used the straightening iron to make my hair as smooth as silk.

I arrived via my coachman and chariot—Lee and his car—and walked into the synagogue. I felt the shivers because the previous year, at that time, Amanda and I were not only volunteering at this party, we were friends as well. A clown greeted me at the door.

"Ah, Queen Esther!"

"Wha?" I blinked.

"Are you as brave as her?" the clown asked.

I stared blankly.

The clown laughed and led me over to a group of girls. Stephanie stood with them.

"Hey, nice hair, math machine!" she said.

I laughed. As I walked toward her, I looked around and noticed that the synagogue was decorated very elegantly. There were long, shiny sheets of gold and silver material draped along the ceiling that fell gracefully onto the floor. There were tables all around the main hall covered with gold tablecloths, and bunches of brightly coloured balloons held in tiny crystal vases as centrepieces. Israeli music was playing, and a bunch of kids dressed in harem costumes were dancing on the dance floor.

Stephanie introduced me to some of the friends she was standing with. One was dressed as a doctor, one was a cowboy, and the other's costume was a complete mystery to me. I was too shy to ask what she was dressed as.

"Sunshine and Moonlight," she confessed to my blank face.

"Oh," I said politely, and I bit into a hamantaschen.

I listened to the conversation between the cowboy and the doctor and decided I totally needed to stop being a hermit and enjoy life. With people! Just as I was starting to enjoy myself, Lisa Amanda, Gail, and David walked into the room. They each wore a bright-coloured sweater with a huge M on it. Ah, I thought. M&M's: My past vice. How appropriate.

Stephanie saw my reaction and took my hand to lead me into a private corner.

"You okay?"

"Not really."

"Are they the friends you used to have?"

"Lucky guess."

"Funny that you dressed as Esther tonight."

"I'm not dressed as Esther," I argued. "I am dressed as an Indian woman. I'm wearing a sari." I felt a little frustrated. *Who was this Esther character, anyway?*

"Well, you look like an Esther."

"Is that why the clown asked me if I was brave?"

"Didn't you go to Sunday School?" Stephanie asked incredulously.

"Sort of."

"Okay, here goes: There was this king, Achashverosh, who wanted to kill the Jews. Queen Esther, his wife who was secretly Jewish, was not at risk and could have done nothing, keeping her identity secret. Instead, she seized the opportunity! She stepped up to the plate and risked her life to help her nation. Her plan worked and she saved her people. She was some queen. Brave as brave could be."

"Okay," I said. "That's cool. But how is this relevant to me?"

"Duh - just like Esther you have the chance to face your enemy, be brave, and deal with the issue. By doing so, may I add, you are at risk, not of death, but of some serious embarrassment!" Stephanie said.

"Feels like death. But you don't know what they did to me." I said.

"Oh, yes I do."

"How?"

"Hello? I go to your school," she said. "I hear the intercom, too." She paused, gauging my reaction. "I saw you eat your lunch in the bathroom."

"Nooooo," I said, feeling incredibly embarrassed.

"You know, there is a reason why we both see Mr. Drane at the ghastly hour in the morning. G-d ISN'T stupid."

"Oh, give me a break," I said.

"Laugh all you want."

"Why should I talk to them?" I asked her, trying to change the subject.

"Why shouldn't you?"

"What are you, my shrink?"

"No, but that would be fun," she laughed.

"Don't get me started."

"Look, sometimes G-d gives us these challenges so we can grow," Stephanie said.

"At this point, I should be a tree."

She laughed. "What would happen if you went to talk to them?"

"I don't know."

"Well, you could forget about it and get on with your life."

"That would be too easy."

"Bingo."

"Okay," I said, and took a deep breath.

I marched up to them. "Hi."

"Hi," Amanda said. Lisa and Gail smiled. David raised his hand to wave.

Silence.

"So. Funny that we're here again, eh?" I began. "A year later. And we're not even religious!"

"Yeah," Lisa agreed.

Gail grinned without showing her teeth.

I couldn't take it anymore, so I walked back to Stephanie. She handed me a cup of punch.

"At least you tried," she said.

I took strong gulps as I took it all in.

Chapter 35

After almost a full year of riding an emotional roller coaster, my math exam was now all I had time for. It was all I had the energy to conquer. I threw my problems with LAG off the table because I had one goal and one goal only: To pass grade nine math.

Lee and I sat in the kitchen with a stack of my old math tests, midterms, and a calculator.

"What, you can't do it all in your head?" I joked as Lee punched numbers into the calculator.

"I need to be accurate for this type of stuff," he said, punching away.

"Uh-huh," I said, tapping my fingers on the table.

Tap, tap, tap.

Tap, tap, tap.

Tap, tap, tap.

"Okay, here it is," Lee finally announced.

My eyes popped open in anticipation as he lay down the calculator and looked up at me.

"Eighty-four percent," he said plainly.

I nearly died. "I need an eighty-four percent mark to pass?" I screeched.

"Yup."

I sank into my chair.

"How the heck am I going to do that?"

Lee shook his head.

"I'll get you the scissors."

"Why?"

"You've got your work cut out for you... come on Lizzie, you can do this. You know you can."

"I don't know," I said in a whisper.

The next morning in Mr. Drane's math clinic, Stephanie and I were busy scratching our pencils into our math workbooks.

"I need an eighty-four," I told her.

"Eighty-nine over here," she stated matter-of-factly.

"Let's go for a run after school today," I suggested.

She stopped what she was doing and stared at me as if I'd just told her that my after-school job was as a stripper.

"Come on," I said. "You took me to your Purim thing; now let me take you to my jogging thing."

"A run could do you good, Stephanie," Mr. Drane piped in.

Stephanie just stared at me with her mouth open, paused, thought about it, smiled, and agreed.

* * *

As soon as I got home that afternoon, I quickly changed and ran to meet Stephanie at our neighbourhood park.

"Let's go!" I yelled with my fists in the air as I ran towards her.

I started with my usual pace and then started to pick up speed as the cool spring air entered my lungs.

"Stephanie? Stephanie?" I said, looking around. I turned around and she was at least a block behind me, waving for me to slow down. I ran to meet her.

"Sorry, I forgot what it's like," I said apologetically.

"It's okay. I just never really run," she said, breathing heavily and holding her side. I instructed her to take deep breaths and to stretch out her side. Once she felt better, we started to jog slowly. Just like I had done when I started with Lee.

We jogged in silence. It kind of felt awkward because I wasn't used to running with anyone other than Lee. I had to say something.

"It feels good to get outside."

"Yeah," Stephanie said breathlessly.

"Clear our minds."

"Yeah."

"To rid ourselves of what's bothering us."

"Yeah."

We paused.

"So, have you called Amanda, Gail, and Lisa yet?" she asked.

I stopped running.

"What's going on here?" I asked.

"Nothing. Just want to know."

"No, I haven't," I said, and started to run again, faster. But Stephanie kept up with my pace.

"What about Jimmy?" she asked.

"How do you know about him?" I asked.

"I have eyes."

"Geez, you're like the FBI."

She laughed.

"No," I said. "I can't think about that stuff right now, all I can think about is passing this course."

"I get it. It's okay," she reassured me.

We jogged the rest of the way in silence.

When we reached the park, she collapsed on the grass while I stretched my legs.

"You killed me," she gasped.

"Oh, goodie. We'll do it again," I said, standing over her. She lifted up her head and gave me the same look she had given me in class that morning.

"Trust me, it will help," I said. "Just please, for now while I'm focusing on math, keep my personal life out of our conversations, okay?"

She nodded.

We went our separate ways, and I spent the rest of the evening going over parabolas.

* * *

"Can't walk," Stephanie said the next morning in our math clinic, rubbing her legs.

"You should have stretched," I chided.

"I've got a trick to teach you about graphs," she said with a twinkle in her eye.

My eyes widened.

She showed me her trick while Mr. Drane supervised.

Stephanie turned to me. "It's my way of saying sorry about butting in yesterday."

I smiled.

"Hey, whatcha doin' this Friday night?" Stephanie asked. "Want to come over for Shabbat?" Her eyes were beaming.

"Who, me?" I said. "Oh. I don't know."

"Oh come on. What else do you have planned? You've got to take a break from the math books sometime!"

I knew she was right, but the thought of going to an orthodox house for Shabbat made me feel a little uncomfortable. I had never been to one before, and all I could picture were scenes from *Fiddler on the Roof*. I didn't know what to expect, but Stephanie was waiting for an answer and I was busy saying "umm."

"Oh, for crying out loud, go!" Mr. Drane said.

"Do you have to put your two cents into everything we do?" I asked.

"Yes," he laughed. "There's got to be some sort of perk for tutoring you girls at the crack of dawn every day."

"Okay," I said. "I'll come."

"We're religious, not freaks. You'll be fine!" Stephanie said, and she dashed off to class.

My mind immediately went to Jimmy and the time I had gone to his house for Shabbat, which instantly made me smile.

* * *

Friday night arrived, and since it was a beautiful spring evening and she lived a few blocks away, I decided to walk to her place. As I walked up the pathway, I noticed how large her house was, with two huge white columns standing by the front door. I rang the bell.

"You're not supposed to wing the bell! It's Shabbos!" yelled a little girl of about five who answered the door. All I could do was smile back at her because she was so cute, with her huge, brown, almond eyes and big chubby cheeks that flushed after she spoke.

"All right, all right, Olivia," Stephanie said as she came running to the front door. "It's not Shabbat yet, sweetie. We have about forty-five minutes." Olivia ran into the hallway, but not before sticking her tongue out at me.

"Little sisters," Stephanie began.

"Don't got one, but she's too cute!" I said, taking off my jacket.

"Yeah, she can be." Stephanie took my coat and hung it up in the closet. We walked into the kitchen.

"Welcome, welcome!" said a lady who seemed a few years older than my mother.

"Ma, this is Lizzie," Stephanie said. "Lizzie, this is my mother."

"Pleased to meet you. Thank you for having me for Shabbat," I said a little too politely.

"Anyone who is up at the crack of dawn with my daughter, trying to pass a math exam, is a friend of mine!" the woman said as she arranged a tray of potatoes. I laughed in agreement, feeling a little more at ease.

"Would you like a glass of wine, Lizzie, dear?"

"No thanks," I said. I was flattered that she had offered, but I felt too shy to accept.

"Whew, it's hot in here," she said, fanning herself. "Or it may be my new sheitel. Either that, or I'm going through menopause!"

"It's the hot potatoes, Ma," Stephanie said while she picked a cucumber slice from a tossed salad and popped it in her mouth.

"Stephanie, go get me a vase from the living room," came a woman's voice from behind a cupboard. The woman then popped her head up to see me.

"Oh, hi!" she said. "I'm Stephanie's sister, Amalia." I smiled.

"I don't see any flowers, ding-but," Stephanie joked.

"Oh, there will be. Phillip is coming tonight," she said.

"Oh, in that case…" Stephanie said, motioning for me to follow her. "Her fiancé," she whispered in explanation.

As we walked into the living room, I gasped at all of the beautiful paintings and lavish furniture. All we had in our house were family portraits, although we did have a Picasso print in our kitchen, which I thought was super-fancy.

"Hmm," Stephanie said as she pondered the array of vases that were carefully placed in a dark cherry-wood cupboard.

"I like this one," I said, trying to be helpful.

"Good choice," Stephanie said. She picked up the vase with both hands and held it like a newborn baby. We walked back to the kitchen.

"You picked the one I schlepped from Prague," Stephanie's mother said.

"This calls for a little glass of wine!" Stephanie announced. This time, I accepted.

So, I was a cheap drunk. How was I to know that one glass of wine was going to make me so happy—then woozy, then dizzy, and then nauseated?

"You okay, Lizzie?" Stephanie asked me, between the fourth and fifth courses.

"Oh yeah, sure," I said. I suddenly felt the urge to visit some ceramic.

"Upstairs and to the left," Stephanie's father said.

As I broke my perfect record of being vomit-free since age eleven, I heard a knock at the door.

It was Stephanie's sister's fiancé, Phillip.

"They did this to me the first time I came for Shabbat. Almost like an initiation," he said as he handed me a glass of water.

After I drank the water and took a few deep breaths, I returned to the table, feeling a little bit better.

"So, you guys are burning the midnight oil for math, eh?" Stephanie's father said.

"Burning an entire olive oil factory," I said.

"Peanut oil," Stephanie said.

"Sunflower," I said.

Stephanie's father shook his head and smiled.

Stephanie and Philip walked me home after dinner. I climbed into bed that night smiling because I had found my partner in crime.

* * *

The next morning, I was in my PJs, watching Bugs Bunny and eating my bagel, cream cheese, and lox sandwich. I was happy as a pig in its poop. Then the phone rang. I didn't answer it.

"It's Jimmy," my mother said, standing in her bathrobe, coffee in one hand and the telephone in the other. She was giving me a you'd-better-deal-with-this look. I nodded for her to give me the phone.

"Bugs?" Jimmy asked.

"Yep," I said.

"Bagel and lox?"

"Don't forget the cream cheese."

He laughed.

I laughed.

We spoke for about five minutes. I told him about my Shabbat dinner and my broken vomit-free record. He told me I was a cheap date. He asked me to go for a walk later on in the afternoon. I told him I wasn't ready yet.

But then I was. Two weeks after that Saturday morning, I sat in the very same spot, eating the same thing: a bagel, cream cheese, and lox sandwich. The phone rang again, but this time I answered it. Jimmy asked to go for a walk and I accepted.

The minute I hung up the phone, I dashed to the bathroom to shower and get dressed. I was too excited and too nervous to straighten my hair, so I threw on my jeans and an old sweatshirt. My hands were too shaky to even attempt to put on mascara. As I walked to the park to meet him, I found an old lip gloss in my jeans, so I put some on as I walked.

We met at the swings. It was so good to see him outside of school. He looked great, and I just wanted to hug him.

I sat on a swing and he pushed me. Then I jumped off and ran towards the wading pool, which was not yet opened for summer. Jimmy ran after me.

"Hey! How did you get so fast?" he yelled as he caught up with me.

"Running has been keeping me sane," I said breathlessly.

We both stopped running and stood, at opposite sides of the wading pool, staring at each other. He walked closer to me and reached out to hold me at my waist. I stared into his eyes and I stood on my tippy-toes to kiss him. He let go of my waist and moved his hands to my back as I reconnected with him.

* * *

A week before the big exam, I had a private tutoring session with Mr. Drane after school. He had fire in his eyes and was sweating all around his forehead while he explained more equations, slopes, and word problems. After a while, Mr. Drane put down his math helmet and gave me a few words of encouragement:

"Eat a good breakfast."

"Check."

"Take deep breaths on your way to school. Listen to your iPod.

"Yup."

"Don't talk to anyone on your way to school or the night before."

"Right-o!"

"Write the exam twice."

"Twice?"

He explained that all of his top students wrote their exams twice. They all ask for a separate piece of scrap paper and write the exam again so that they can see the exam as a fresh start instead of going over mistakes again. I thought about it. I decided that at that point, I was willing to try anything.

By the time school ended that afternoon I was in a daze, so I decided to walk home. I was happy to see Lee sitting in the kitchen reading the sports section of the newspaper.

"Hey," I said, and sat down across from him.

"Hi," he said, still reading.

I stared a hole through his newspaper.

"What's up?" he asked, finally looking up at me.

"Do you have to ask?" I said glumly.

"You'll do fine."

"Easy for you to say. You always do fine."

He frowned.

"It's not fair. Math comes so easy for you."

"I can't help it. I like it."

"You don't have to rub it in."

"Look, you've been working your butt off," he said. "You know your stuff, and it will pay off."

"I need to go for a run."

And we ran. And I was fast. I couldn't believe that Lee was panting right beside me.

"Would it be so bad if you failed?" he asked.

"Well, they would put me back, just for math."

"Is that so bad?"

"Math is an elective once you get to grade eleven," I mused. "So it would all even out."

"See? No biggie."

"Yeah," I agreed.

It all made sense, but it didn't sit right. I could blow it off and try again next year, but all my hard work that I have been doing would go down the drain. I couldn't give up. I had to give it my best shot.

"Just give it your best shot," Lee said as we turned the corner.

Lee had just read my mind.

We finished our run in silence and approached our front door.

"Wait for me in the kitchen," he said.

He came back five minutes later with a bunch of his grade nine math tests. I wrote all of them as Lee poured water into my glass and answered any questions I had. Someone must have put "patient pills" in his orange juice that morning.

Chapter 36

It was the night before the exam. I soaked my stressed and extremely nervous body in a steaming hot bubble bath and watched a really stupid reality show on TV. I called Jimmy to tell him how stupid it was and how nervous I was.

"You'll do fine."

"I hate that word: fine. Yech."

"Okay, you'll do great?"

"I'm gonna kick ass."

"Kick ass, it is."

I called Stephanie.

"May our hard work pay off," Stephanie said.

"Did you go running today?" I asked.

"I went for a brisk walk. It totally relaxed me."

"It's a start."

"Yeah."

"Hey, thanks for being there, these past two months. Really helped."

"Ditto."

"I'm going to say a special prayer for us."

"Pray away," I laughed.

As I put on my PJs, I decided that I was ready to put on my scuba suit and go swimming with the sharks the next morning.

On exam day, I awoke at 6:30. I was calm, even a bit excited. My parents were at my bedroom door, peeking in to see how I'd slept, and they were relieved to see that my complexion was normal and not white or green. I went for a quick jog with Lee, hopped into the shower, and had my usual bowl of Raisin Bran with berries and milk. I brushed my teeth and gave each family member a hug, and then left to conquer the mountain of math.

As I waited outside the exam room I saw Mrs. Sherwood approach, and a huge smile swept across my face—*she* was facilitating the exam! Even though I had only had her in grade seven, she was one of my favourite teachers in the school. There was something about her that always made me feel at ease, so her monitoring—I was convinced—was a gift from G-d. We both said hello, and I was the first one to follow her into the classroom to take a seat.

Amanda sat in front of me. She turned around to say hello and I said "Hi" back. Then the exam papers were distributed. As mine was placed in front of my nose, I asked Mrs. Sherwood for an extra piece of paper and to my surprise, I was not the only one who asked.

"You may begin," Mrs. Sherwood announced.

After a full hour I had finished the exam. It seemed to go smoothly, except for the fact that I had "Bennie and the Jets" by Elton John stuck in my head. Nevertheless, I could still concentrate, and things just seemed to add up (no pun intended).

Eventually, Mrs. Sherwood announced, "Students, you may be dismissed."

I felt Amanda's eyes on my head. I looked up at her and smiled. She smiled back and got up to leave with three-quarters of the class.

I could have left as well, but according to my plan, I was only half-finished. I put my exam away and started again on a fresh piece of paper. When I finished my second version, I compared it with my original and realized that I had made a few careless mistakes! I took a deep breath and corrected them. When that was all done, I lifted my head to discover that I was the only person left in the classroom.

I got up and handed Mrs. Sherwood my exam paper. I felt relieved and scared at the same time. After I walked out of the classroom and closed the door behind me, I fell to my knees, crunched down like a ball and said aloud, "I can't believe it's over." Mrs. Sherwood opened the door, walked around my body, and bent down to ask me if I was alright. I lifted my head and said, "Never better." I got up and left. As I approached the front doors of the school, Jimmy was there, sitting on the steps.

"How'd it go?"

"I think it went okay."

He smiled.

"How long were you sitting here?"

"It doesn't matter."

I walked up to hug him.

"There's something to be said for someone with so much perseverance," he said as he kissed my head.

I looked up.

"I know it's hard for you to be around people like me and your brother. Other kids who get it so easy."

A tear ran down my cheek.

"It means so much more if you aced the exam than if I did," he whispered into my ear.

* * *

With the big exam over, there was nothing left to do but pray and wait for my results. Besides, camp was in two weeks and since I had gone down two sizes, I had some serious shopping to do.

I also had to go to Frieda's for my final weigh-in before I left for camp. I did not go for several weeks. Actually, make that over a month.

"Lizzie! Where have you been?" squealed one of the weigh-in ladies.

"School. Exams. Stuff," I admitted while I got on the scale.

"Oh my G-d," she squealed again.

"Oh my G-d!" I squealed myself.

"You did it!"

"I got to my goal!"

I got off the scale stunned as I took my seat. The leader of the group asked me to speak about how I did it. I got up, scanned the audience, and said: "Perseverance."

Several nights later, I ran into Mr. Drane at a restaurant around the corner from my house. My eyes popped out of my head when he came through the front doors with his family. I went up to him and said hello. They all looked like they drew geometry figures for fun.

"Oh, you're Lizzie," his wife said.

"Yeah, that's me."

"You worked really hard, eh?"

"You're telling me. But, thanks to Mr. Drane… Well, when will I find out?" I asked.

"In due time, Lizzie."

"But when?"

"About ten days."

"Ten days! I can't wait that long!"

"I know."

My eyes fell on his family. I couldn't help but think about Mr. Drane's eldest son, Jeff, and how old he would have been. They all seemed to be happy, but something was missing in their eyes, which put everything into perspective.

"Okay. I'll sit tight."

"Have a great summer."

"Thanks, Mr. Drane … for everything."

I went to see Marna for the last time. We said our good-byes, and I gave her a huge hug and thanked her for helping me through a very tough year. She told me that I could call her during the summer if I needed her and that I should continue seeing her when I got back, but not as often. I agreed.

That afternoon I started to pack. I managed to get all of my grooming stuff in one cosmetic bag, which I was very proud about.

The phone rang.

"Can I come over?" Jimmy asked.

We sat on the floor of my room and leaned against my huge, pink, stuffed dog.

"I still have your shirt—the one you gave me last February," I said.
"Keep it."
"Will you write me a letter?"
"Promise. Will you write me back?"
"While holding your T-shirt."

Epilogue

I loved being back at my second home, camp. My bed was right near Emily's, and our cabin was a great mix of kids.

The best part of all was the sports. It felt great to play soccer and run after the ball and not feel winded. I could play tennis longer and run to catch the ball that was at the other end of the court. Aside from my swim strokes, which needed practicing, I was able to do way more laps than what I could do last year. *Why didn't I take up running sooner?*

I still hadn't heard about my exam.

I saw Paul Liss, my boyfriend from last summer, at the camp opening dance.

"Lizzie! What happened to you?"

I winked at him.

"Wanna dance?"

"Not really, thanks."

I walked away making sure he got a good look at my behind. In my new jeans: two sizes smaller. The rest of the evening, I was busy telling my counsellor about Jimmy.

The next night during dinner, my head counsellor, Wendy, came up to me and said, "Phone call." Everyone in my cabin became quiet. They knew what phone call I was waiting for.

I jumped up to run to the phones in the back of the kitchen. Wendy yelled, "No running in the dining hall!" I ignored her and kept on running. I picked up the receiver. My mom was on the phone.

"Hello?"

"You did it!"

"I what?"

"You got ninety-three percent!"

I screamed out of pure joy, ran to the dining hall, held my hands up in the air, and yelled: "I did it!"

The whole camp cheered, and my bunk got up from their seats and tackled me with hugs. I squirmed up from their bodies and ran back to the dangling phone, where my parents were yelling for me. I told them that I loved them and that I would call back tomorrow. I came back to my table crying and laughing at the same time.

A little while later, Wendy came back to my table. "Phone call," she said again. This time I walked over to the phone. I had no clue who it could be. Maybe my grandmother, my aunt, or even Marna? I picked up the phone and said hello.

It was Mr. Drane!

"Congratulations, Lizzie."

"Thank you."

"You know, you taught me something, too."

"What could I have possibly taught you?"

"When you have a student who wants to learn, anything is possible. My wife and I started talking about Jeff. We had never really addressed it before and now we are. It feels wonderful."

"There was a reason why I came to your math clinic, Mr. Drane."

I couldn't believe I'd just said that. My smile was so bright that my cheeks were burning.

* * *

The second week of camp, I finally came back to earth. I was in the middle of a tennis competition with the camp across the lake when I received two letters. The first one was a post card from Israel. It read:

"I DID IT. U? Will Be Home in 2 WKS. XOXO, S."

I was elated.

The second one was from Amanda. It wasn't as short as Stephanie's, or as cheery either.

Dear Lizzie,

I hope you are having a blast at camp. I am too. Mainly because it's great being away from all of the yelling, screaming, and stupid lawyers interviewing me with the most ridiculous questions.

Speaking of questions, why this letter? Firstly, I want to congratulate you. Your mom ran into my mom at a yoga class and broke the great news that you aced the math exam. I am so happy for you. You deserve this victory more than anyone.

As for the second reason for this letter: to apologize. I know I tried to say I was sorry several months ago, but this time, I really mean it. I am truly sorry for how I treated you.

Why did I do it? Well, my shrink says I was so angry and confused at home, that I had to get my feelings out on something, on someone—which, unfortunately, turned out to be you, my friend who always, no matter what, was there for me.

As for Gail and Lisa, I can't speak for them, but I know for sure that they still love you and miss you. They were just following me, which was a stupid thing for them to do. I hope they realize that.

When I get home from camp, I'm going to keep seeing this shrink. That will help me get through this lovely period in my life, which my parents created.

You don't have to write me back. Just think about what I wrote and we can talk about it when you get home.

Love,

Amanda.

"What are you going to do?" Emily asked after I read the letter to her.

"Gonna deal with it all when I get home."

"What about Gail and Lisa?" she asked.

"Good question."

That night during dinner, Wendy said, "Telephone again." My whole cabin laughed as I walked back to the kitchen.

I picked up the receiver. Jimmy's voice. "Hello?"

"Where are my letters?" I teased.

"Coming, coming. Where's mine?"

"I've been very busy with tennis."

"Sure, sure." he laughed.

I paused.

"I sleep with your T-shirt every night," I confessed.

"I sleep with the thought of you, every night."

I grinned so loud I'm sure he could hear.

"I got the good news." he said.

I wanted to crawl inside the telephone wires and hug him. But instead, I told him how I really felt.

"I… I love you."

THE END

About the Author

Sharon Neiss — Arbess grew up in Montreal and received her Bachelor of Arts degree from Concordia University's Communications Studies program. After working as a copywriter in advertising for several years, the writing bug bit Sharon on her right hand and lead her to the local coffee shop to write stories of "teen drama" with a little bit of humour.

My So-Called Friends and Me is a story that is entirely fiction, written with the hopes to teach young readers that no matter how bad it gets, you too will come out on the other side, stronger and smarter, with the help of the unexpected to get you through it all.

Neiss-Arbess lives in Toronto with her husband, Gordie and her three children, Josh, Adam, and Olivia. In addition to being an author, Neiss-Arbess is the the co-publisher of Day Ja View, The Ultimate Family Calendar.

SHARON NEISS ARBESS

CPSIA information can be obtained at www.ICGtesting.com
Printed in the USA
LVOW07s0137061115

461154LV00014B/91/P